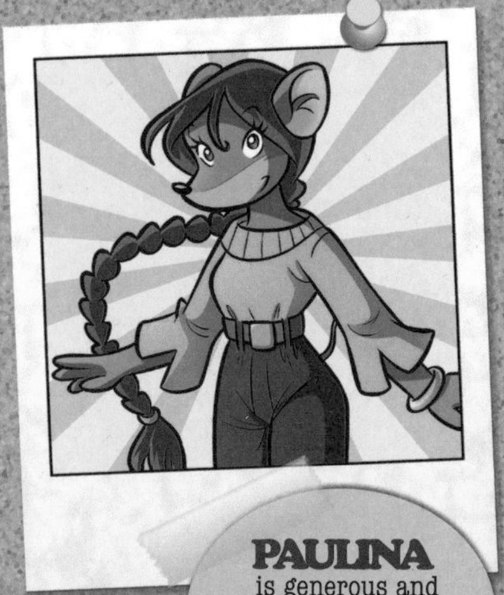

PAULINA
is generous and optimistic. She likes traveling and meeting people from all over the world.

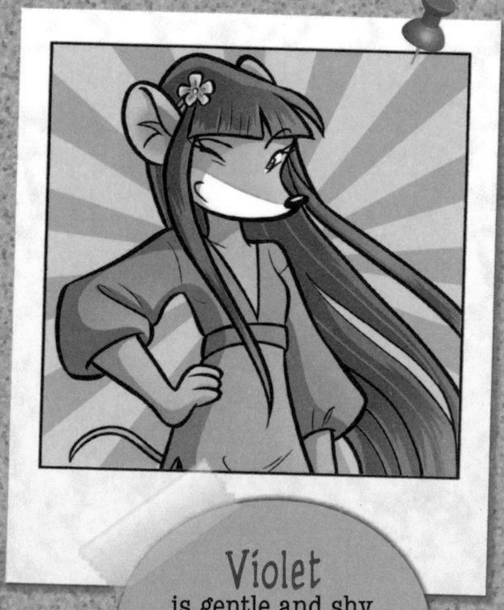

Violet
is gentle and shy. Because of this, she can be taken to be a bit of a snobby rodent.

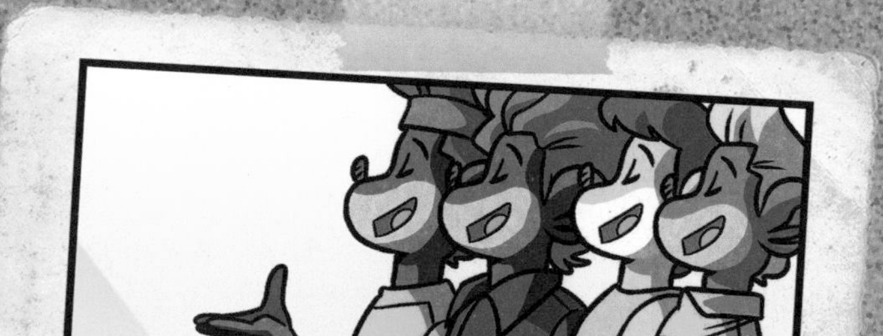

Global singing sensation **6 SECONDS OF SPRING** is visiting Whale Island for a charity concert. They are also judging the **Mouseford Academy** talent contest. Will they find their opening act among the students?

Thea Stilton

PAPERCUT**Z**™

Thea Stilton

A SONG FOR THE THEA SISTERS

by Thea Stilton

PAPERCUTZ™

New York

THEA STILTON #7
A SONG FOR THE THEA SISTERS
Geronimo Stilton and Thea Stilton names, characters and related indicia are copyright,
trademark, and exclusive license of Atlantyca S.p.A.
All rights reserved.
The moral right of the author has been asserted.

Text by Thea Stilton
Cover by Ryan Jampole
Editorial supervision by Alessandra Berello and Chiara Richelmi (Atlantyca S.p.A.)
Script by Francesco Savino
Translation by Nanette McGuinness
Art by Ryan Jampole
Color by Laurie E. Smith
Lettering by Wilson Ramos Jr.

Based on an original idea by Elisabetta Dami

© Atlantyca S.p.A. – via Leopardi 8, 20123 Milano, Italia – foreignrights@atlantyca.it
© 2017 for this Work in English language by Papercutz, 160 Broadway, Suite 700, East
Wing, New York, NY 10038

www.geronimostilton.com

Stilton is a name of a famous English cheese. It is a registered trademark of the Stilton
Cheese Markers' Association.
For more information go to www.stiltoncheese.com

Production – Dawn Guzzo
Production Coordinator – Sasha Kimiatek
Assistant Managing Editor – Jeff Whitman
Jim Salicrup
Editor-in-Chief

ISBN: 978-162991-640-8

Printed in China
March 2017

Papercutz books may be purchased for business or promotional use.
For information on bulk purchases, please contact Macmillan Corporate and Premium
Sales Department at (800) 221-7945 x5442.
Distributed by Macmillan
First Printing

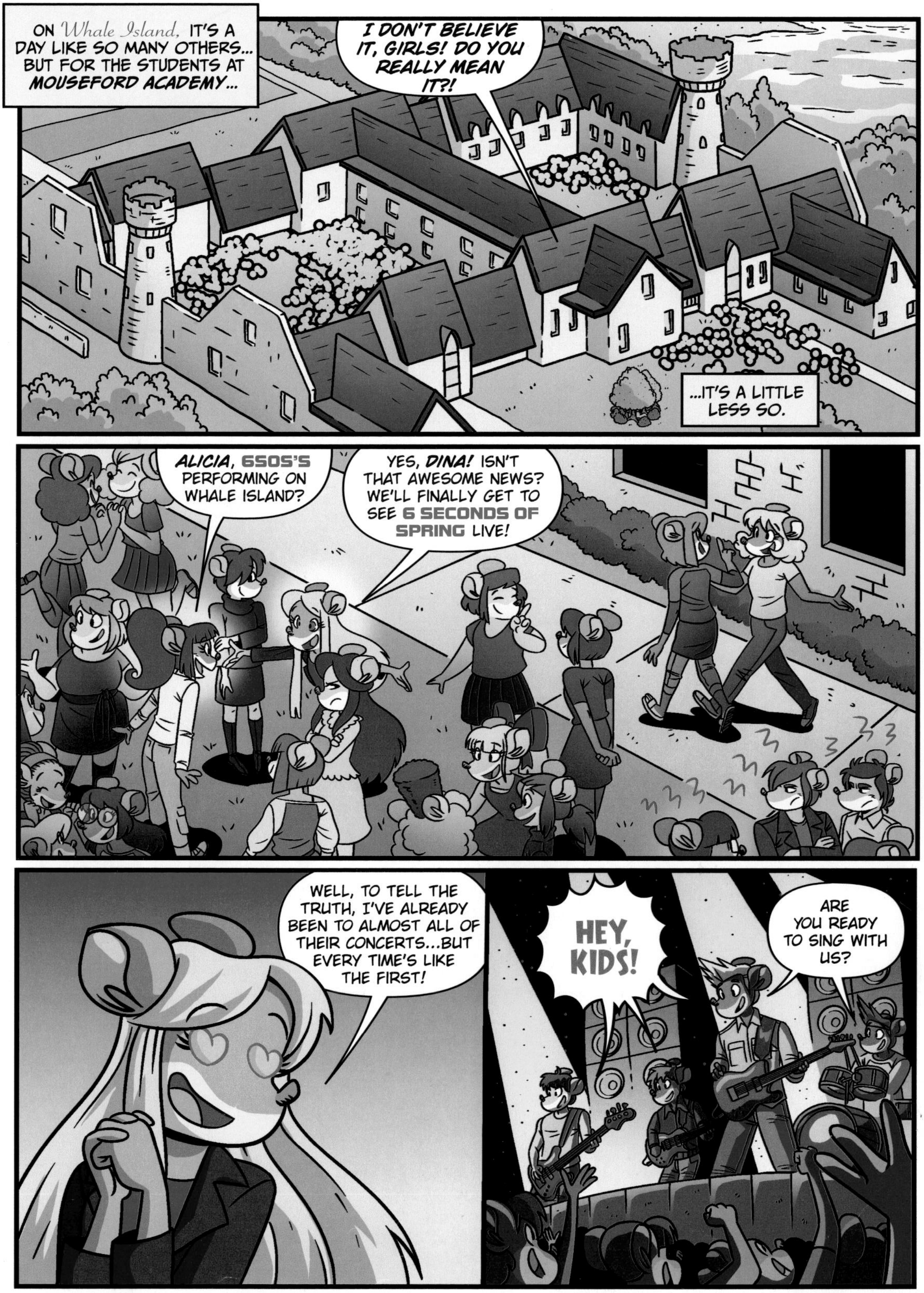

ON Whale Island, IT'S A DAY LIKE SO MANY OTHERS... BUT FOR THE STUDENTS AT MOUSEFORD ACADEMY...
I DON'T BELIEVE IT, GIRLS! DO YOU REALLY MEAN IT?!
...IT'S A LITTLE LESS SO.
ALICIA, 6SOS'S PERFORMING ON WHALE ISLAND?
YES, DINA! ISN'T THAT AWESOME NEWS? WE'LL FINALLY GET TO SEE 6 SECONDS OF SPRING LIVE!
WELL, TO TELL THE TRUTH, I'VE ALREADY BEEN TO ALMOST ALL OF THEIR CONCERTS...BUT EVERY TIME'S LIKE THE FIRST!
HEY, KIDS!
ARE YOU READY TO SING WITH US?

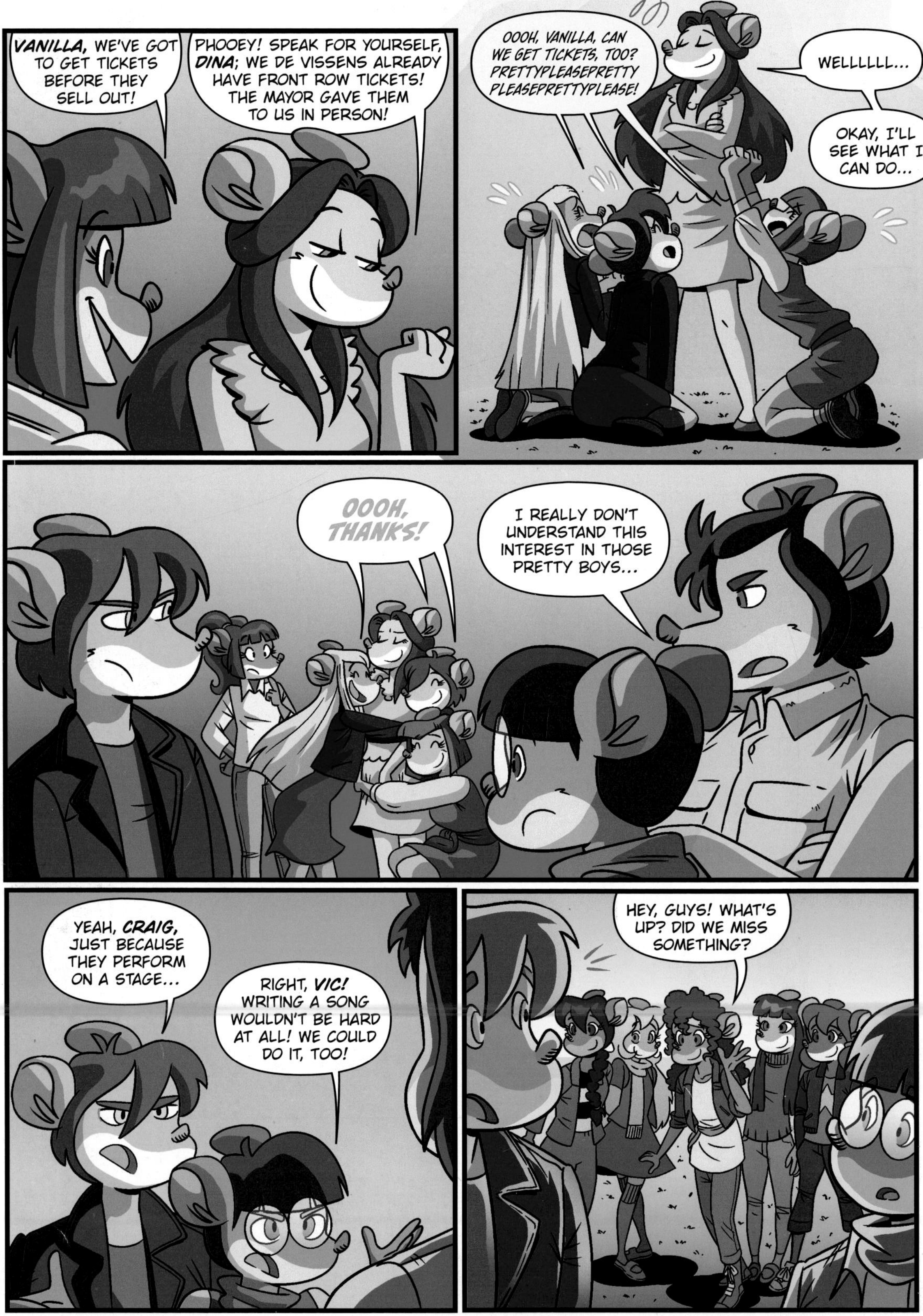

VANILLA, WE'VE GOT TO GET TICKETS BEFORE THEY SELL OUT!
PHOOEY! SPEAK FOR YOURSELF, DINA; WE DE VISSENS ALREADY HAVE FRONT ROW TICKETS! THE MAYOR GAVE THEM TO US IN PERSON!
OOOH, VANILLA, CAN WE GET TICKETS, TOO? PRETTYPLEASEPRETTY PLEASEPRETTYPLEASE!
WELLLLLL...
OKAY, I'LL SEE WHAT I CAN DO...
OOOH, THANKS!
I REALLY DON'T UNDERSTAND THIS INTEREST IN THOSE PRETTY BOYS...
YEAH, CRAIG, JUST BECAUSE THEY PERFORM ON A STAGE...
RIGHT, VIC! WRITING A SONG WOULDN'T BE HARD AT ALL! WE COULD DO IT, TOO!
HEY, GUYS! WHAT'S UP? DID WE MISS SOMETHING?

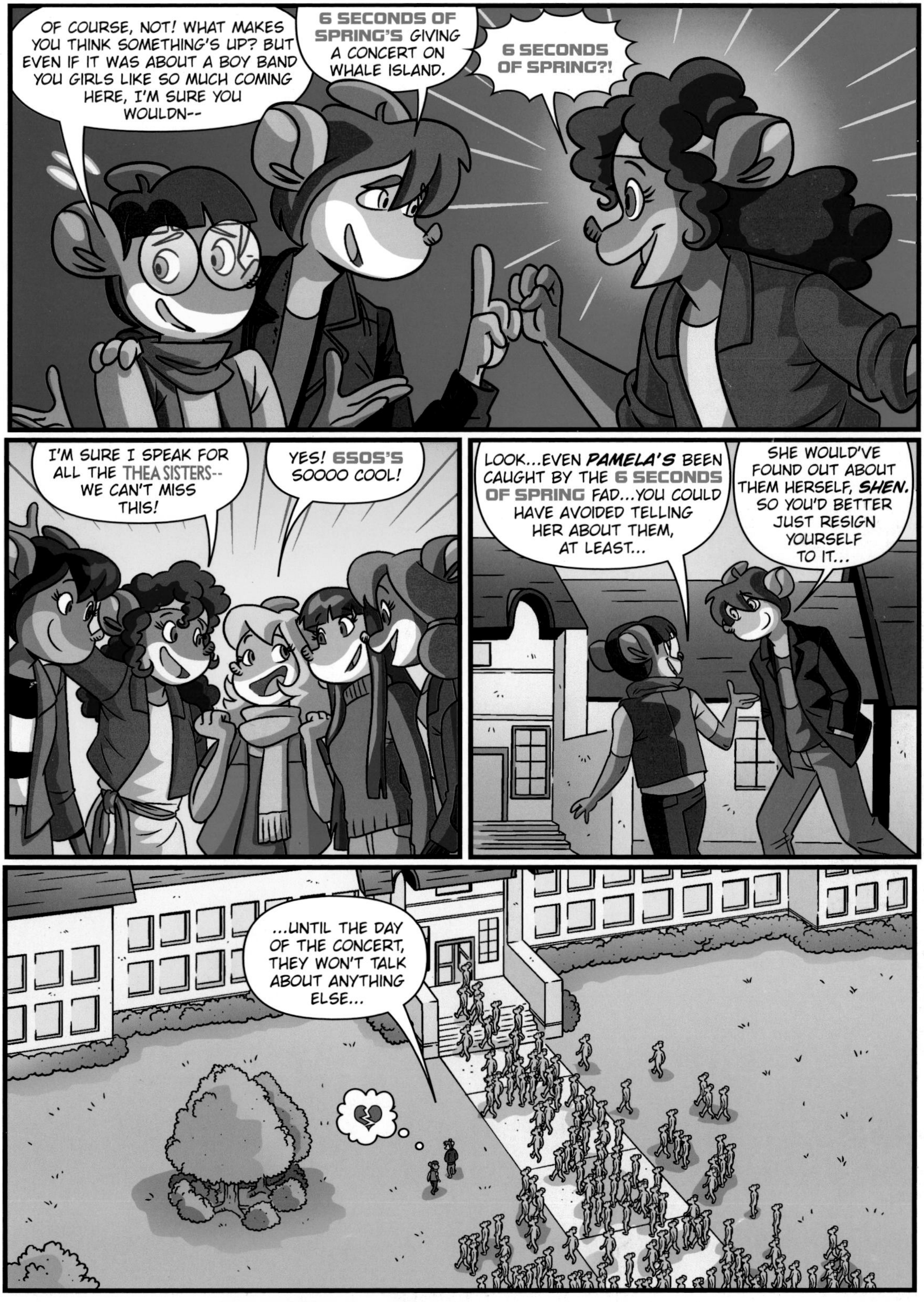
OF COURSE, NOT! WHAT MAKES YOU THINK SOMETHING'S UP? BUT EVEN IF IT WAS ABOUT A BOY BAND YOU GIRLS LIKE SO MUCH COMING HERE, I'M SURE YOU WOULDN--
6 SECONDS OF SPRING'S GIVING A CONCERT ON WHALE ISLAND.
6 SECONDS OF SPRING?!
I'M SURE I SPEAK FOR ALL THE THEA SISTERS-- WE CAN'T MISS THIS!
YES! 6SOS'S SOOOO COOL!
LOOK...EVEN PAMELA'S BEEN CAUGHT BY THE 6 SECONDS OF SPRING FAD...YOU COULD HAVE AVOIDED TELLING HER ABOUT THEM, AT LEAST...
SHE WOULD'VE FOUND OUT ABOUT THEM HERSELF, SHEN. SO YOU'D BETTER JUST RESIGN YOURSELF TO IT...
...UNTIL THE DAY OF THE CONCERT, THEY WON'T TALK ABOUT ANYTHING ELSE...

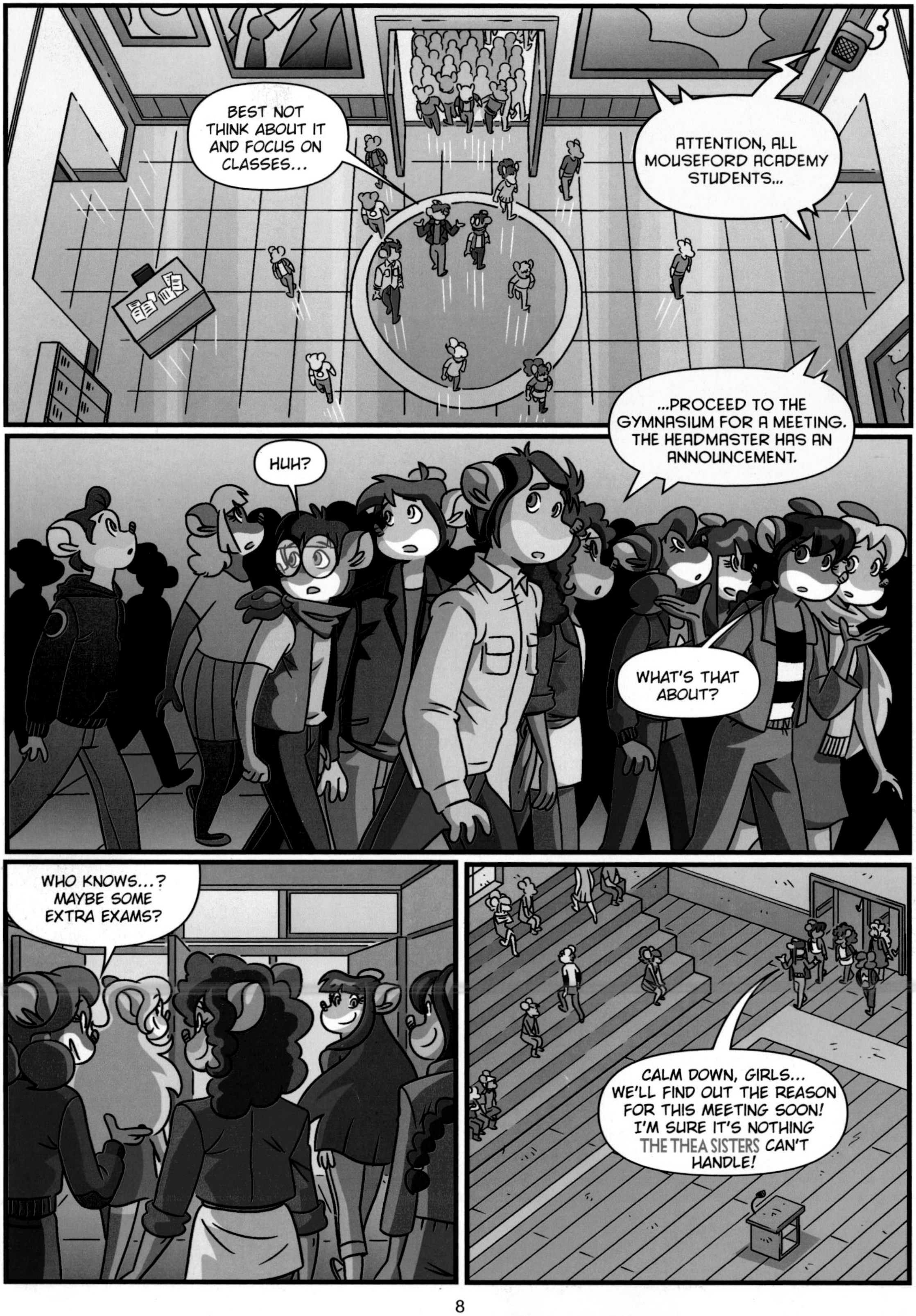
BEST NOT THINK ABOUT IT AND FOCUS ON CLASSES...
ATTENTION, ALL MOUSEFORD ACADEMY STUDENTS...
...PROCEED TO THE GYMNASIUM FOR A MEETING. THE HEADMASTER HAS AN ANNOUNCEMENT.
HUH?
WHAT'S THAT ABOUT?
WHO KNOWS...? MAYBE SOME EXTRA EXAMS?
CALM DOWN, GIRLS... WE'LL FIND OUT THE REASON FOR THIS MEETING SOON! I'M SURE IT'S NOTHING THE THEA SISTERS CAN'T HANDLE!

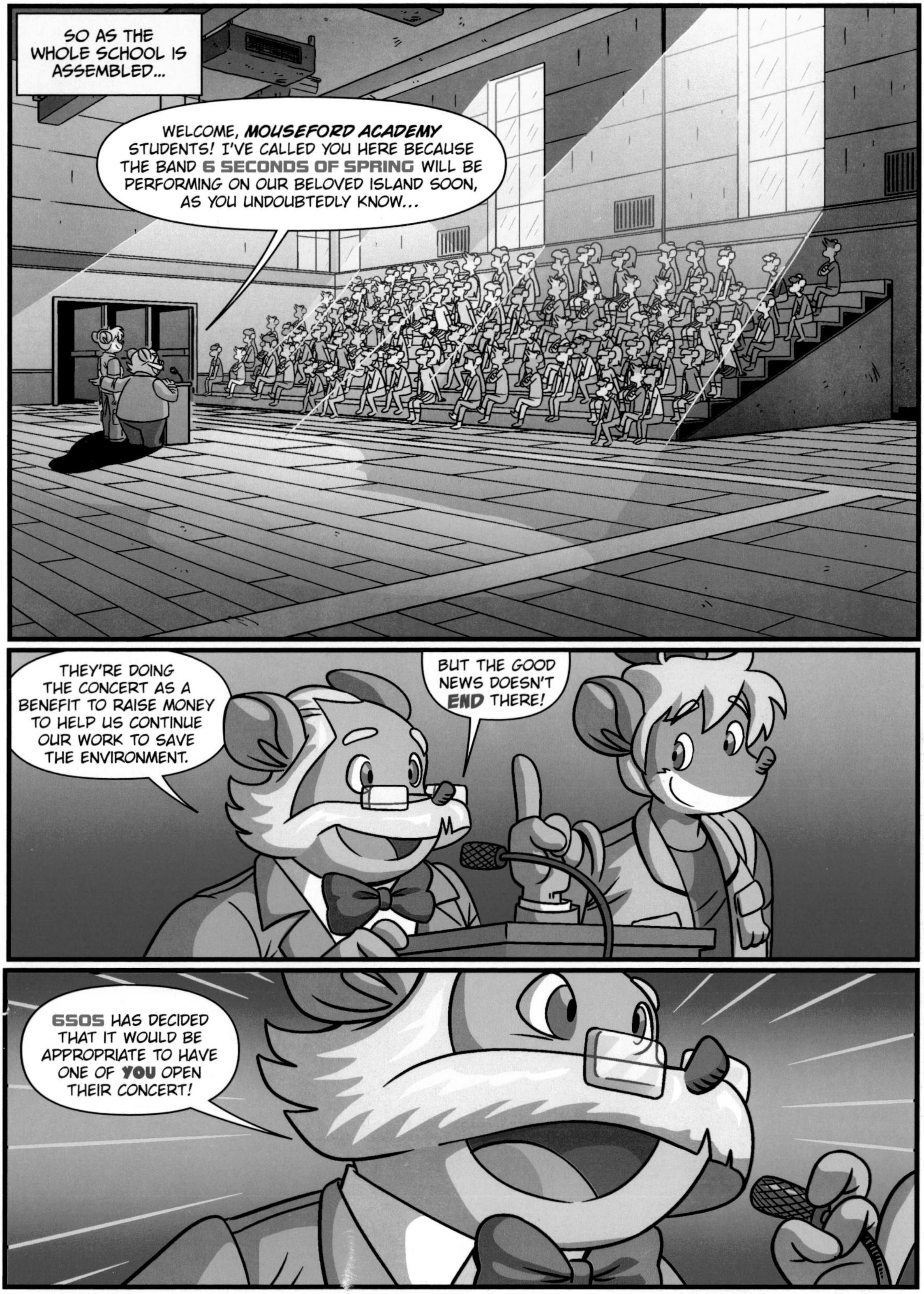
SO AS THE WHOLE SCHOOL IS ASSEMBLED...
WELCOME, MOUSEFORD ACADEMY STUDENTS! I'VE CALLED YOU HERE BECAUSE THE BAND 6 SECONDS OF SPRING WILL BE PERFORMING ON OUR BELOVED ISLAND SOON, AS YOU UNDOUBTEDLY KNOW...
THEY'RE DOING THE CONCERT AS A BENEFIT TO RAISE MONEY TO HELP US CONTINUE OUR WORK TO SAVE THE ENVIRONMENT.
BUT THE GOOD NEWS DOESN'T END THERE!
6SOS HAS DECIDED THAT IT WOULD BE APPROPRIATE TO HAVE ONE OF YOU OPEN THEIR CONCERT!

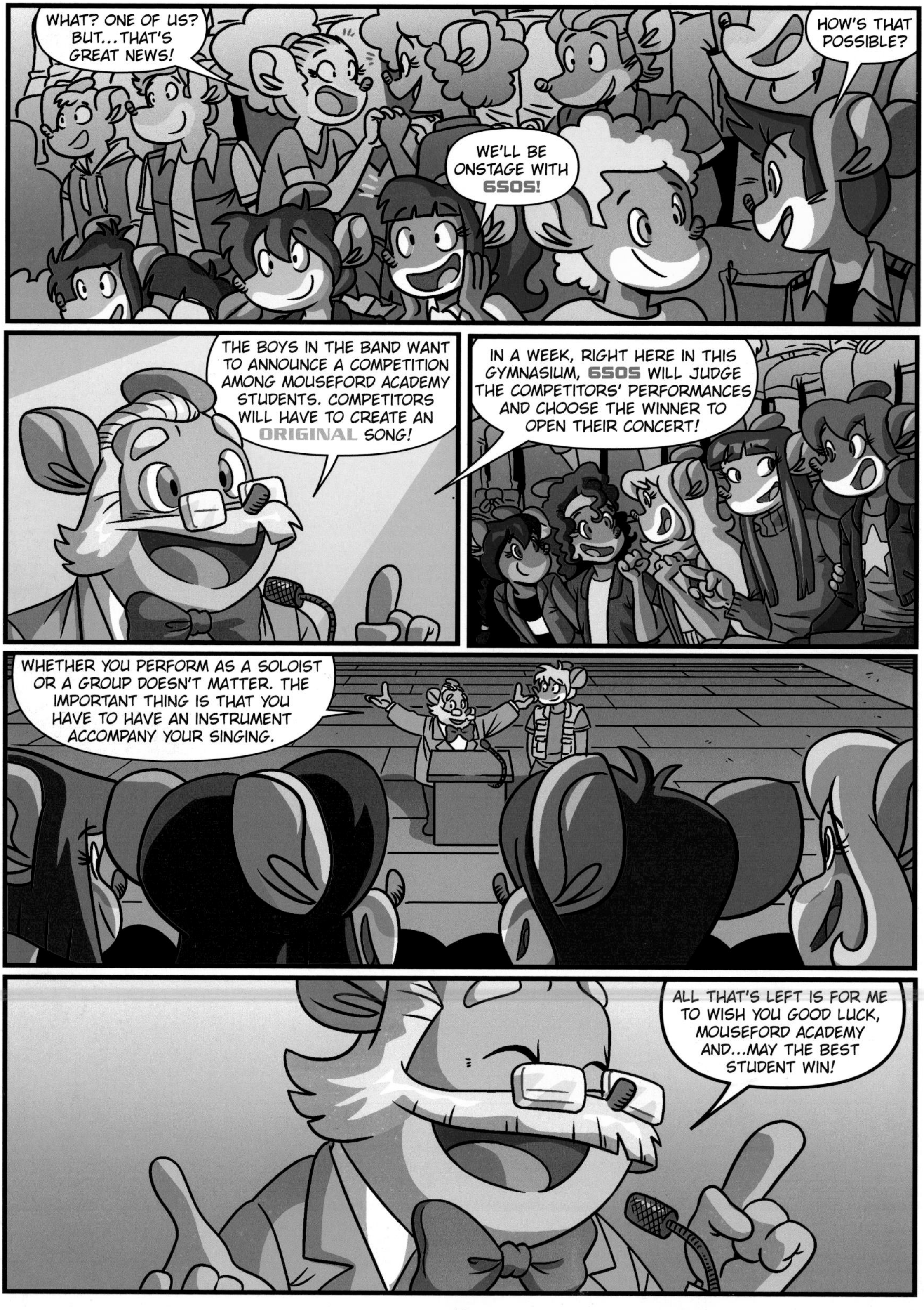
WHAT? ONE OF US? BUT...THAT'S GREAT NEWS!
HOW'S THAT POSSIBLE?
WE'LL BE ONSTAGE WITH 6SOS!
THE BOYS IN THE BAND WANT TO ANNOUNCE A COMPETITION AMONG MOUSEFORD ACADEMY STUDENTS. COMPETITORS WILL HAVE TO CREATE AN ORIGINAL SONG!
IN A WEEK, RIGHT HERE IN THIS GYMNASIUM, 6SOS WILL JUDGE THE COMPETITORS' PERFORMANCES AND CHOOSE THE WINNER TO OPEN THEIR CONCERT!
WHETHER YOU PERFORM AS A SOLOIST OR A GROUP DOESN'T MATTER. THE IMPORTANT THING IS THAT YOU HAVE TO HAVE AN INSTRUMENT ACCOMPANY YOUR SINGING.
ALL THAT'S LEFT IS FOR ME TO WISH YOU GOOD LUCK, MOUSEFORD ACADEMY AND...MAY THE BEST STUDENT WIN!

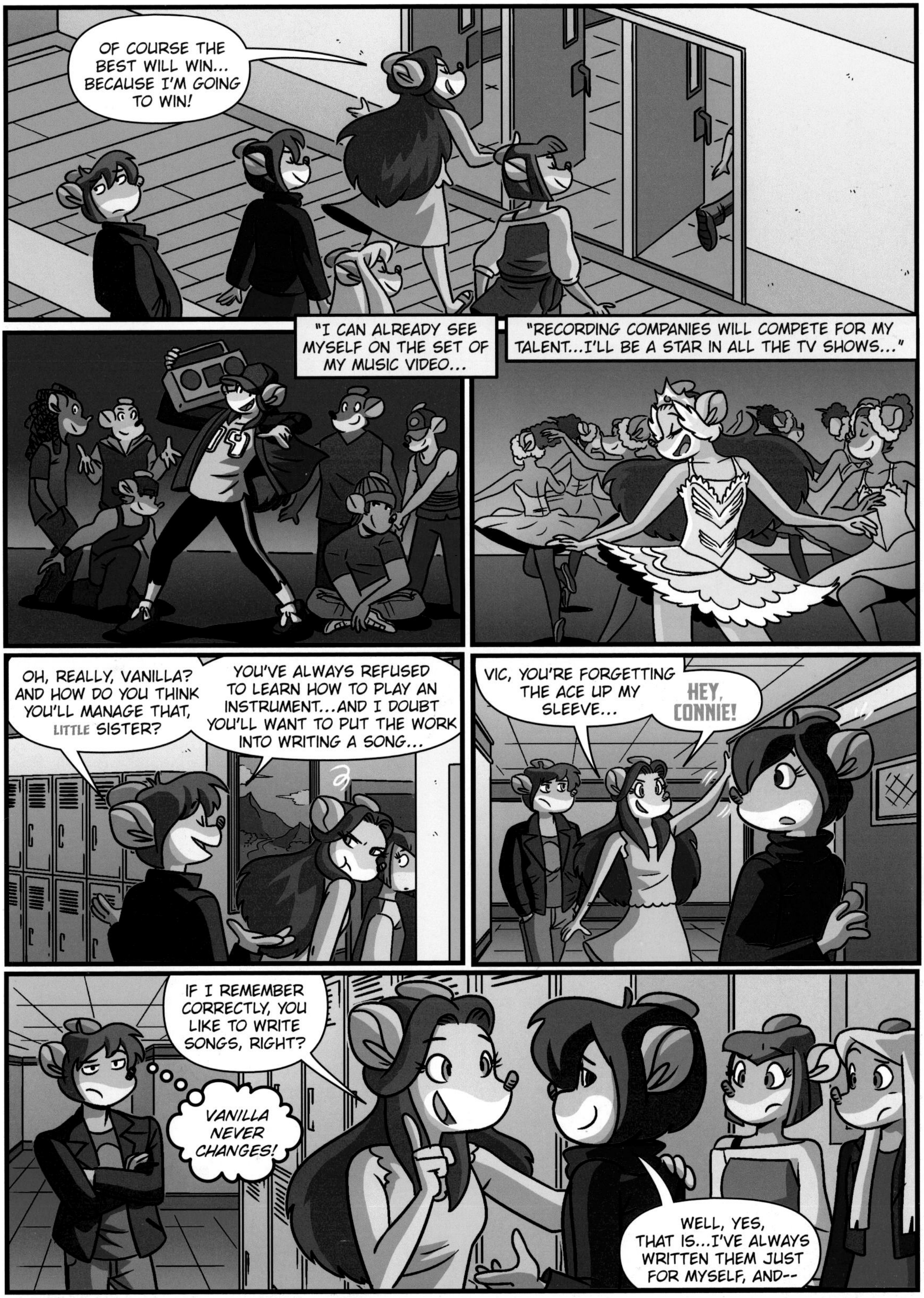

OF COURSE THE BEST WILL WIN... BECAUSE I'M GOING TO WIN!
"I CAN ALREADY SEE MYSELF ON THE SET OF MY MUSIC VIDEO...
"RECORDING COMPANIES WILL COMPETE FOR MY TALENT...I'LL BE A STAR IN ALL THE TV SHOWS..."
OH, REALLY, VANILLA? AND HOW DO YOU THINK YOU'LL MANAGE THAT, LITTLE SISTER?
YOU'VE ALWAYS REFUSED TO LEARN HOW TO PLAY AN INSTRUMENT...AND I DOUBT YOU'LL WANT TO PUT THE WORK INTO WRITING A SONG...
VIC, YOU'RE FORGETTING THE ACE UP MY SLEEVE...
HEY, CONNIE!
IF I REMEMBER CORRECTLY, YOU LIKE TO WRITE SONGS, RIGHT?
VANILLA NEVER CHANGES!
WELL, YES, THAT IS...I'VE ALWAYS WRITTEN THEM JUST FOR MYSELF, AND--

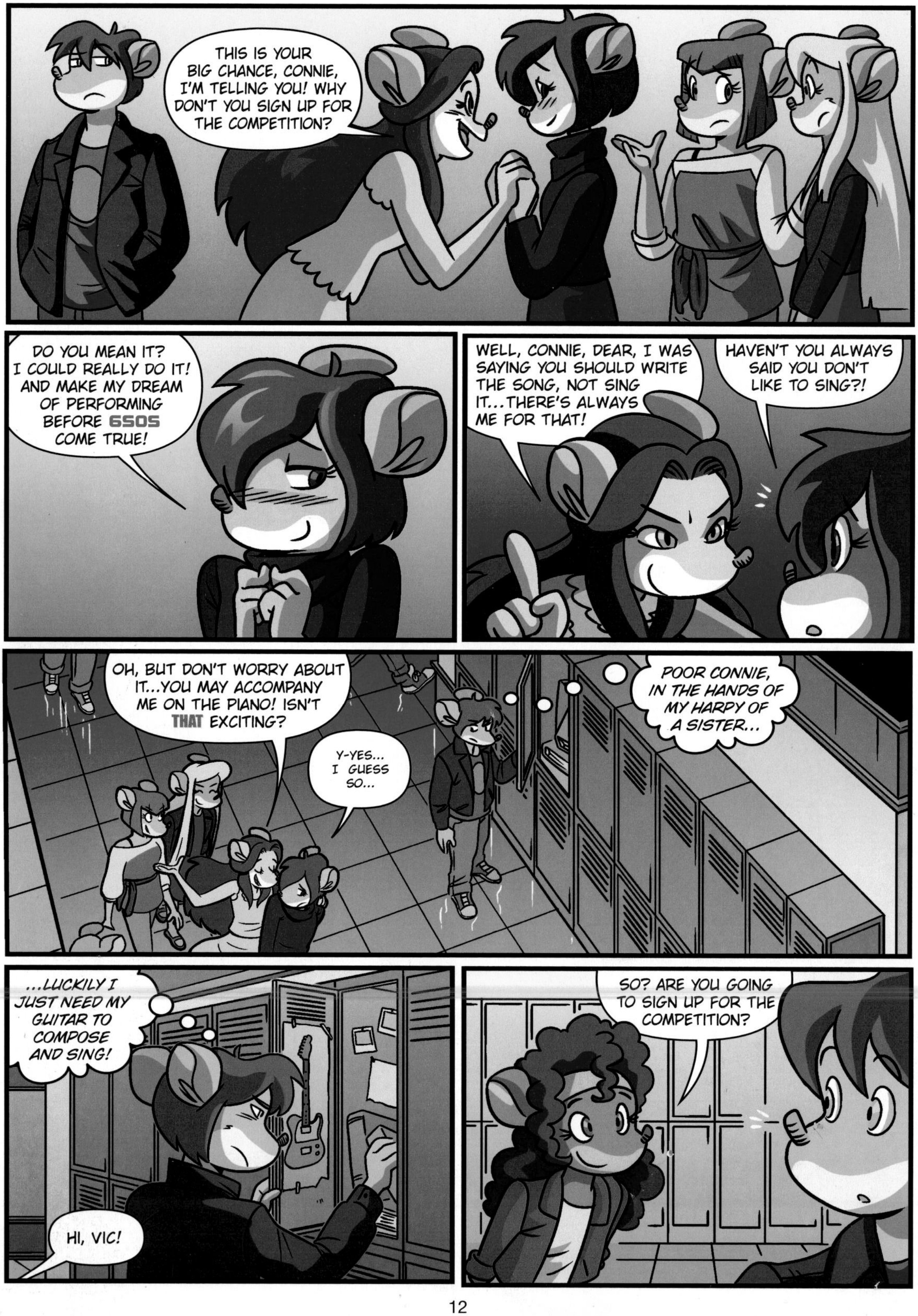
THIS IS YOUR BIG CHANCE, CONNIE, I'M TELLING YOU! WHY DON'T YOU SIGN UP FOR THE COMPETITION?
DO YOU MEAN IT? I COULD REALLY DO IT! AND MAKE MY DREAM OF PERFORMING BEFORE 6SOS COME TRUE!
WELL, CONNIE, DEAR, I WAS SAYING YOU SHOULD WRITE THE SONG, NOT SING IT... THERE'S ALWAYS ME FOR THAT!
HAVEN'T YOU ALWAYS SAID YOU DON'T LIKE TO SING?!
OH, BUT DON'T WORRY ABOUT IT... YOU MAY ACCOMPANY ME ON THE PIANO! ISN'T THAT EXCITING?
Y-YES... I GUESS SO...
POOR CONNIE, IN THE HANDS OF MY HARPY OF A SISTER...
...LUCKILY I JUST NEED MY GUITAR TO COMPOSE AND SING!
HI, VIC!
SO? ARE YOU GOING TO SIGN UP FOR THE COMPETITION?

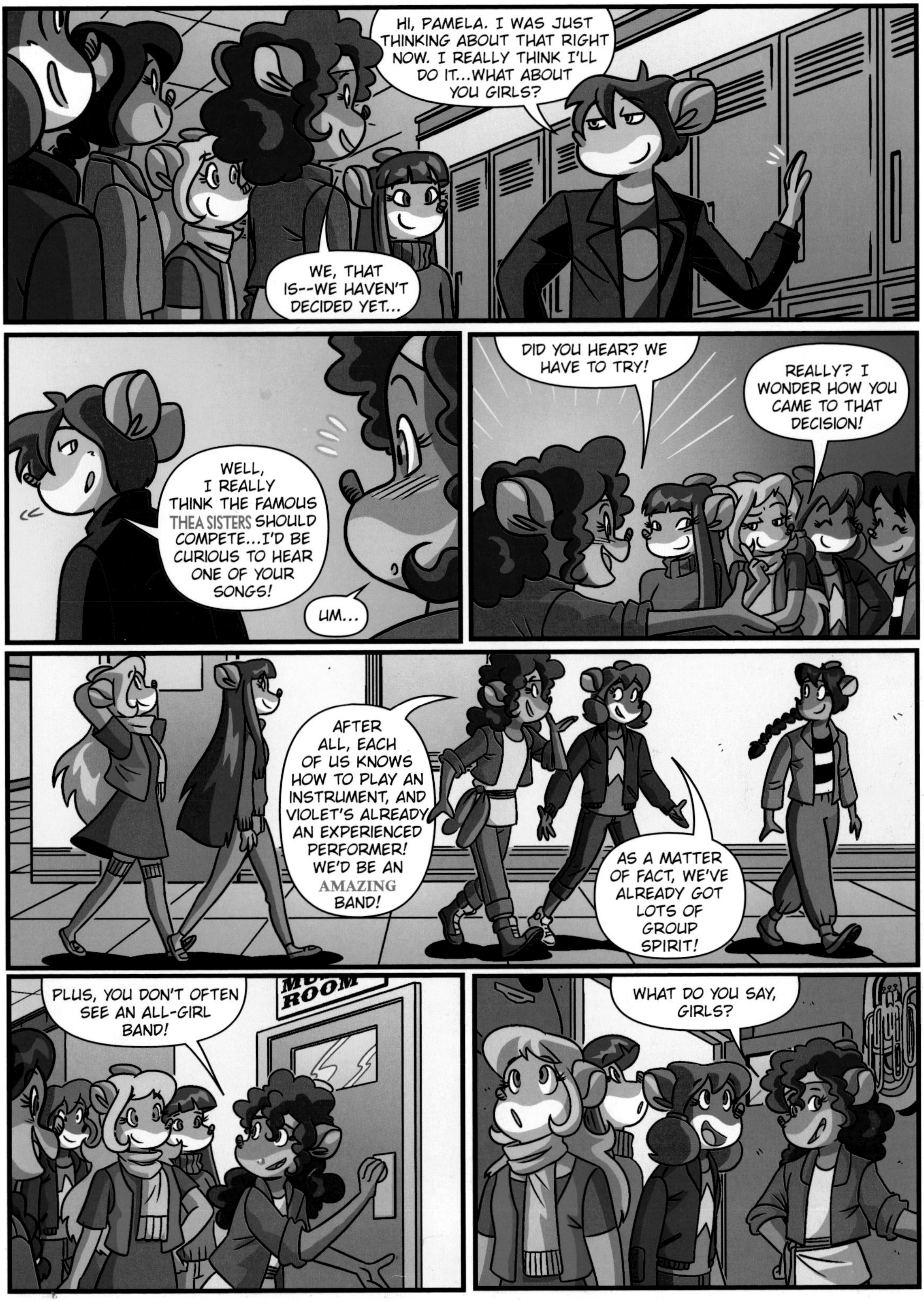
HI, PAMELA. I WAS JUST THINKING ABOUT THAT RIGHT NOW. I REALLY THINK I'LL DO IT...WHAT ABOUT YOU GIRLS?
WE, THAT IS--WE HAVEN'T DECIDED YET...
WELL, I REALLY THINK THE FAMOUS THEA SISTERS SHOULD COMPETE...I'D BE CURIOUS TO HEAR ONE OF YOUR SONGS!
UM...
DID YOU HEAR? WE HAVE TO TRY!
REALLY? I WONDER HOW YOU CAME TO THAT DECISION!
AFTER ALL, EACH OF US KNOWS HOW TO PLAY AN INSTRUMENT, AND VIOLET'S ALREADY AN EXPERIENCED PERFORMER! WE'D BE AN AMAZING BAND!
AS A MATTER OF FACT, WE'VE ALREADY GOT LOTS OF GROUP SPIRIT!
PLUS, YOU DON'T OFTEN SEE AN ALL-GIRL BAND!
ROOM
WHAT DO YOU SAY, GIRLS?

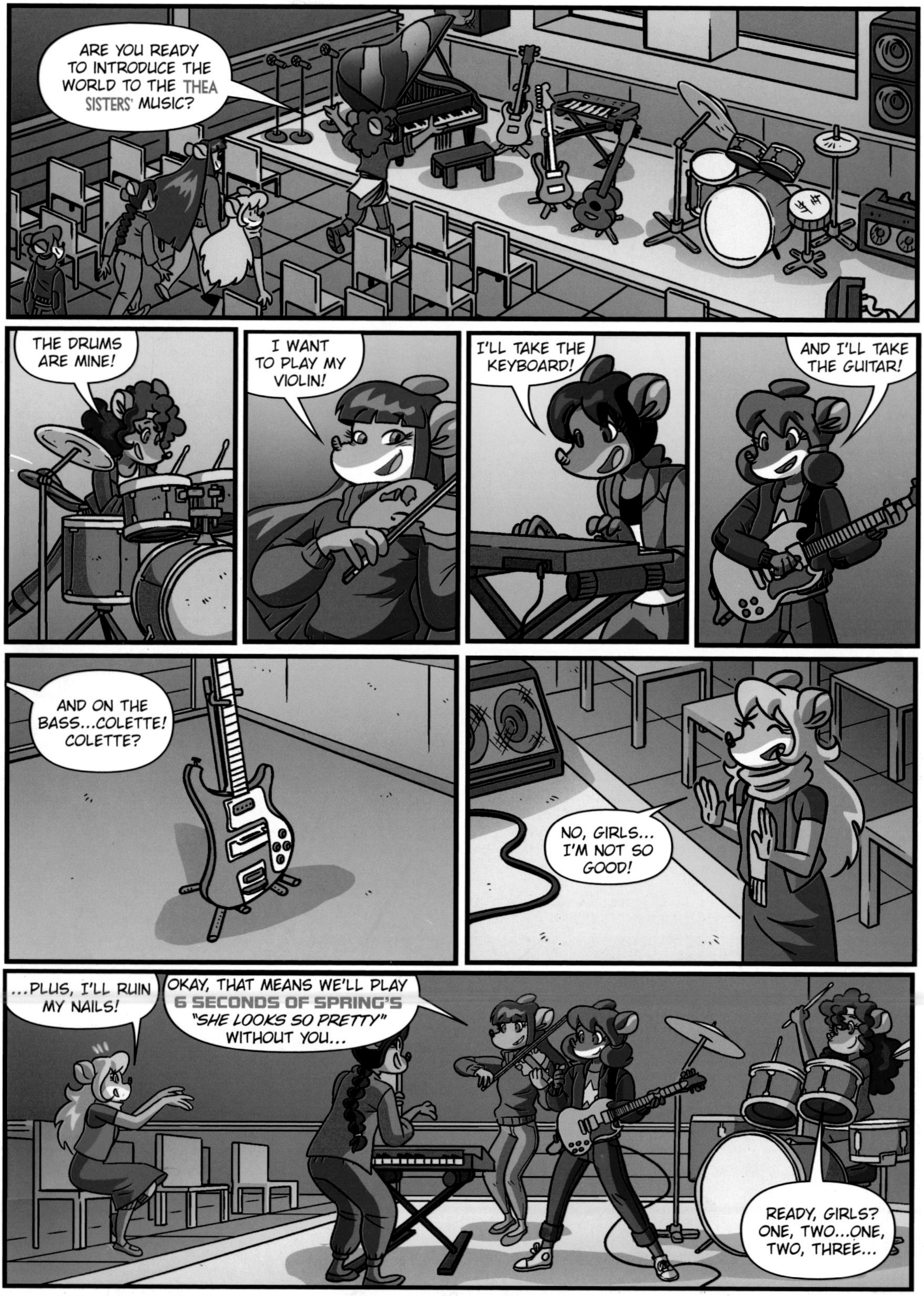
ARE YOU READY TO INTRODUCE THE WORLD TO THE THEA SISTERS' MUSIC?
THE DRUMS ARE MINE!
I WANT TO PLAY MY VIOLIN!
I'LL TAKE THE KEYBOARD!
AND I'LL TAKE THE GUITAR!
AND ON THE BASS...COLETTE! COLETTE?
NO, GIRLS... I'M NOT SO GOOD!
...PLUS, I'LL RUIN MY NAILS!
OKAY, THAT MEANS WE'LL PLAY 6 SECONDS OF SPRING'S "SHE LOOKS SO PRETTY" WITHOUT YOU...
READY, GIRLS? ONE, TWO...ONE, TWO, THREE...

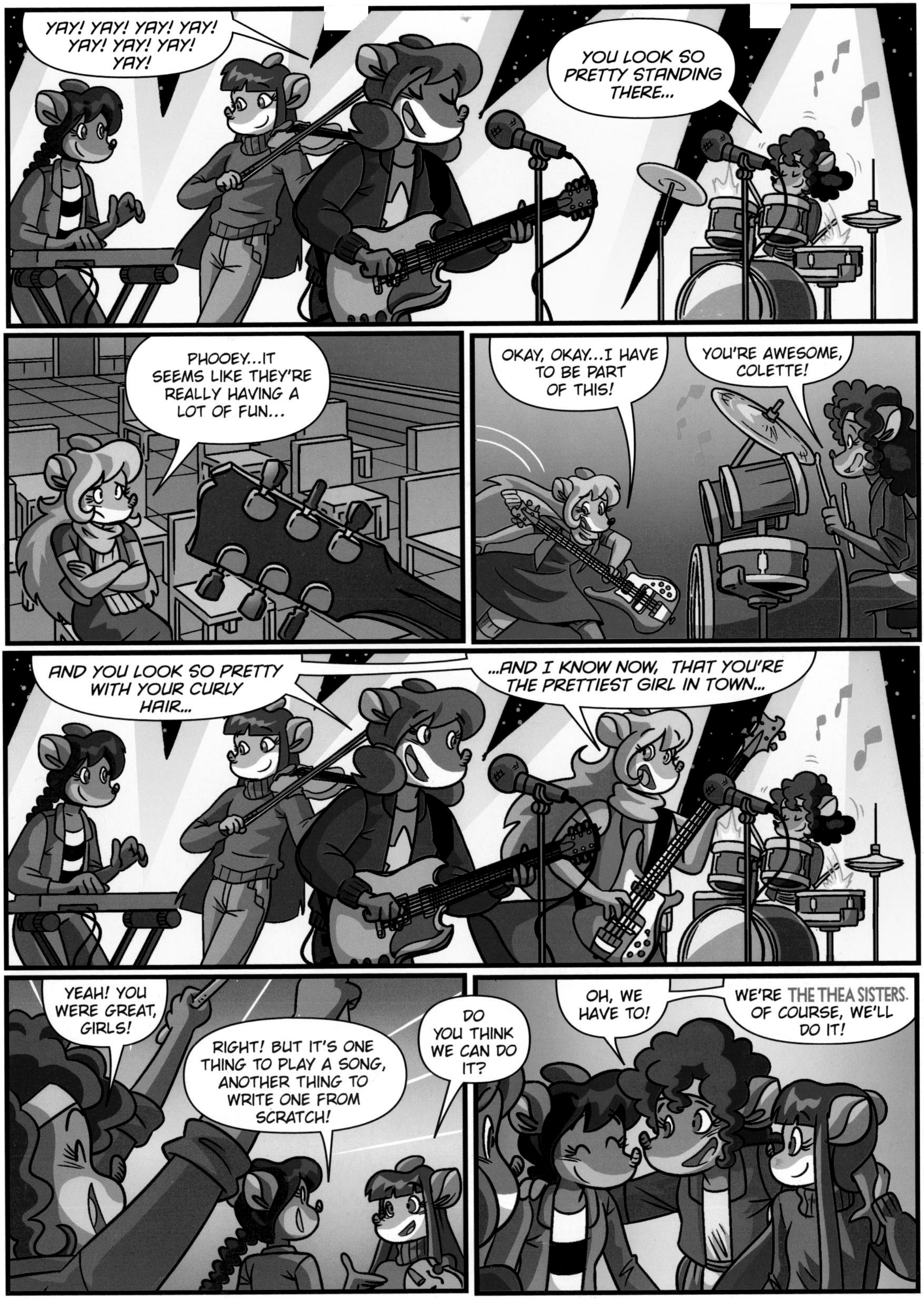
YAY! YAY! YAY! YAY! YAY! YAY! YAY! YAY! YAY!
YOU LOOK SO PRETTY STANDING THERE...
PHOOEY...IT SEEMS LIKE THEY'RE REALLY HAVING A LOT OF FUN...
OKAY, OKAY...I HAVE TO BE PART OF THIS!
YOU'RE AWESOME, COLETTE!
AND YOU LOOK SO PRETTY WITH YOUR CURLY HAIR...
...AND I KNOW NOW, THAT YOU'RE THE PRETTIEST GIRL IN TOWN...
YEAH! YOU WERE GREAT, GIRLS!
RIGHT! BUT IT'S ONE THING TO PLAY A SONG, ANOTHER THING TO WRITE ONE FROM SCRATCH!
DO YOU THINK WE CAN DO IT?
OH, WE HAVE TO!
WE'RE THE THEA SISTERS. OF COURSE, WE'LL DO IT!

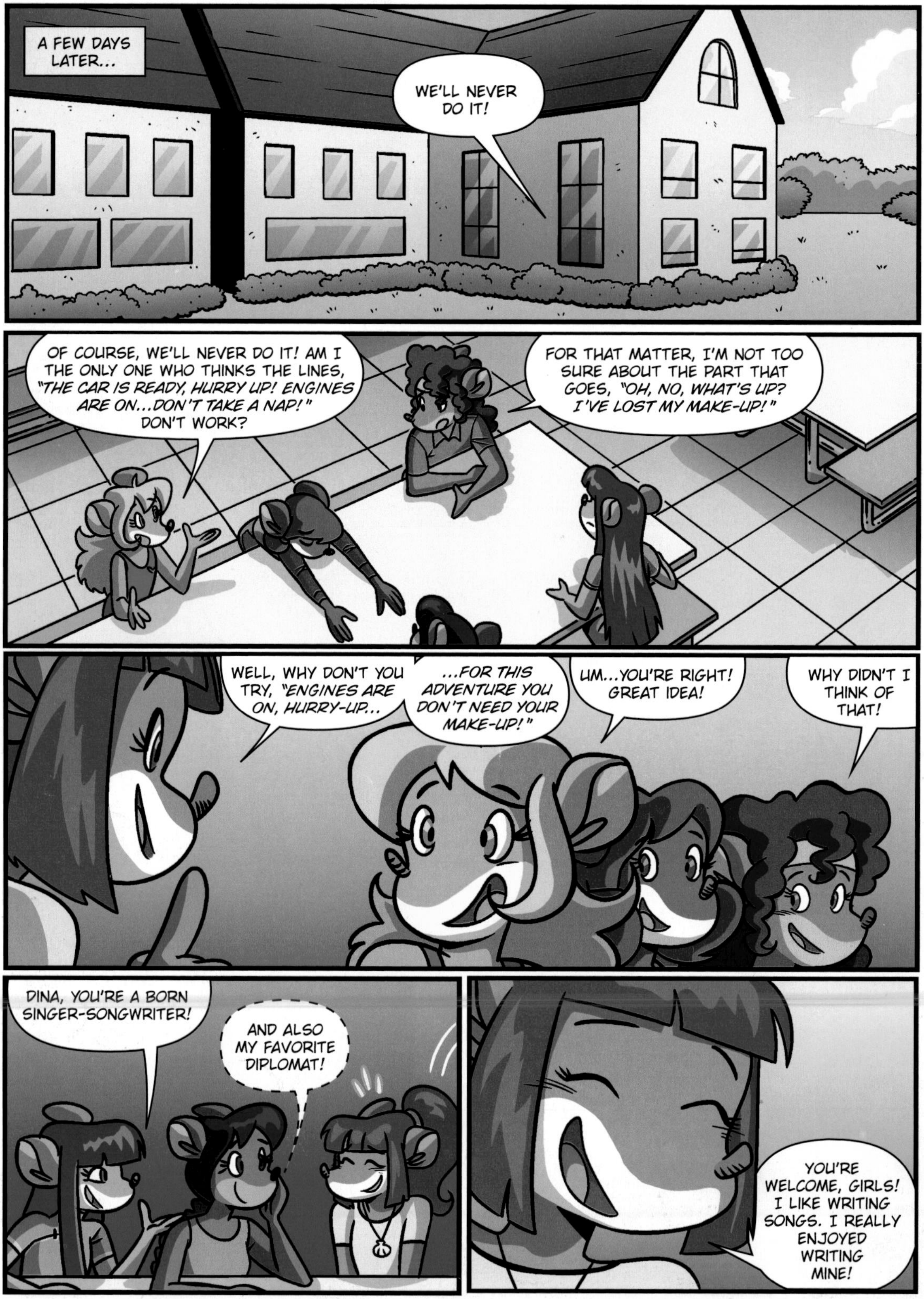

A FEW DAYS LATER...
WE'LL NEVER DO IT!
OF COURSE, WE'LL NEVER DO IT! AM I THE ONLY ONE WHO THINKS THE LINES, "THE CAR IS READY, HURRY UP! ENGINES ARE ON...DON'T TAKE A NAP!" DON'T WORK?
FOR THAT MATTER, I'M NOT TOO SURE ABOUT THE PART THAT GOES, "OH, NO, WHAT'S UP? I'VE LOST MY MAKE-UP!"
WELL, WHY DON'T YOU TRY, "ENGINES ARE ON, HURRY-UP...
...FOR THIS ADVENTURE YOU DON'T NEED YOUR MAKE-UP!"
UM...YOU'RE RIGHT! GREAT IDEA!
WHY DIDN'T I THINK OF THAT!
DINA, YOU'RE A BORN SINGER-SONGWRITER!
AND ALSO MY FAVORITE DIPLOMAT!
YOU'RE WELCOME, GIRLS! I LIKE WRITING SONGS. I REALLY ENJOYED WRITING MINE!

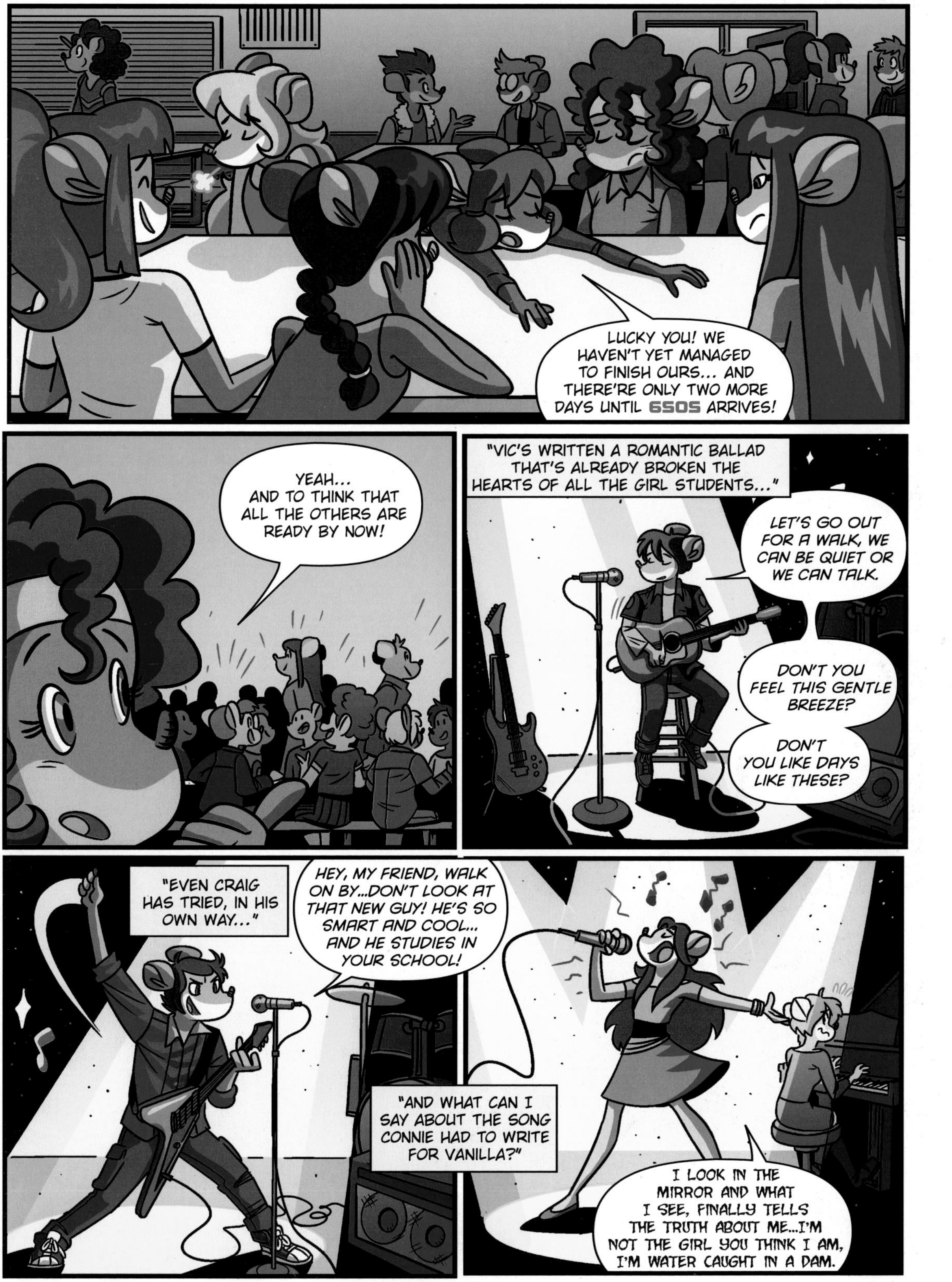

LUCKY YOU! WE HAVEN'T YET MANAGED TO FINISH OURS... AND THERE'RE ONLY TWO MORE DAYS UNTIL 6SOS ARRIVES!
YEAH... AND TO THINK THAT ALL THE OTHERS ARE READY BY NOW!
"VIC'S WRITTEN A ROMANTIC BALLAD THAT'S ALREADY BROKEN THE HEARTS OF ALL THE GIRL STUDENTS..."
LET'S GO OUT FOR A WALK, WE CAN BE QUIET OR WE CAN TALK.
DON'T YOU FEEL THIS GENTLE BREEZE?
DON'T YOU LIKE DAYS LIKE THESE?
"EVEN CRAIG HAS TRIED, IN HIS OWN WAY..."
HEY, MY FRIEND, WALK ON BY...DON'T LOOK AT THAT NEW GUY! HE'S SO SMART AND COOL... AND HE STUDIES IN YOUR SCHOOL!
"AND WHAT CAN I SAY ABOUT THE SONG CONNIE HAD TO WRITE FOR VANILLA?"
I LOOK IN THE MIRROR AND WHAT I SEE, FINALLY TELLS THE TRUTH ABOUT ME...I'M NOT THE GIRL YOU THINK I AM, I'M WATER CAUGHT IN A DAM.

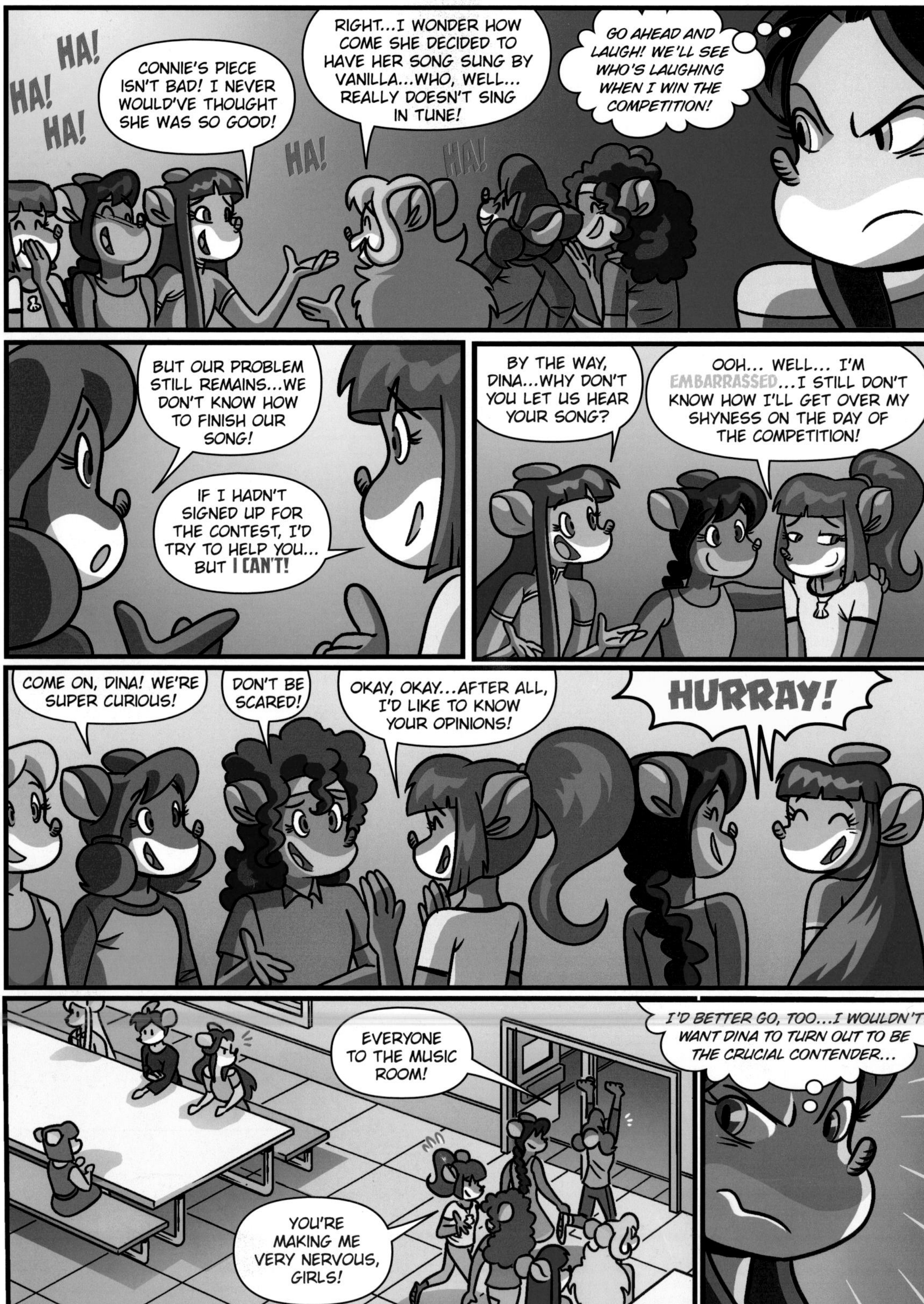
HA! HA! HA!
CONNIE'S PIECE ISN'T BAD! I NEVER WOULD'VE THOUGHT SHE WAS SO GOOD!
RIGHT...I WONDER HOW COME SHE DECIDED TO HAVE HER SONG SUNG BY VANILLA...WHO, WELL... REALLY DOESN'T SING IN TUNE!
HA!
HA!
GO AHEAD AND LAUGH! WE'LL SEE WHO'S LAUGHING WHEN I WIN THE COMPETITION!
BUT OUR PROBLEM STILL REMAINS...WE DON'T KNOW HOW TO FINISH OUR SONG!
IF I HADN'T SIGNED UP FOR THE CONTEST, I'D TRY TO HELP YOU... BUT I CAN'T!
BY THE WAY, DINA...WHY DON'T YOU LET US HEAR YOUR SONG?
OOH... WELL... I'M EMBARRASSED...I STILL DON'T KNOW HOW I'LL GET OVER MY SHYNESS ON THE DAY OF THE COMPETITION!
COME ON, DINA! WE'RE SUPER CURIOUS!
DON'T BE SCARED!
OKAY, OKAY...AFTER ALL, I'D LIKE TO KNOW YOUR OPINIONS!
HURRAY!
EVERYONE TO THE MUSIC ROOM!
YOU'RE MAKING ME VERY NERVOUS, GIRLS!
I'D BETTER GO, TOO...I WOULDN'T WANT DINA TO TURN OUT TO BE THE CRUCIAL CONTENDER...

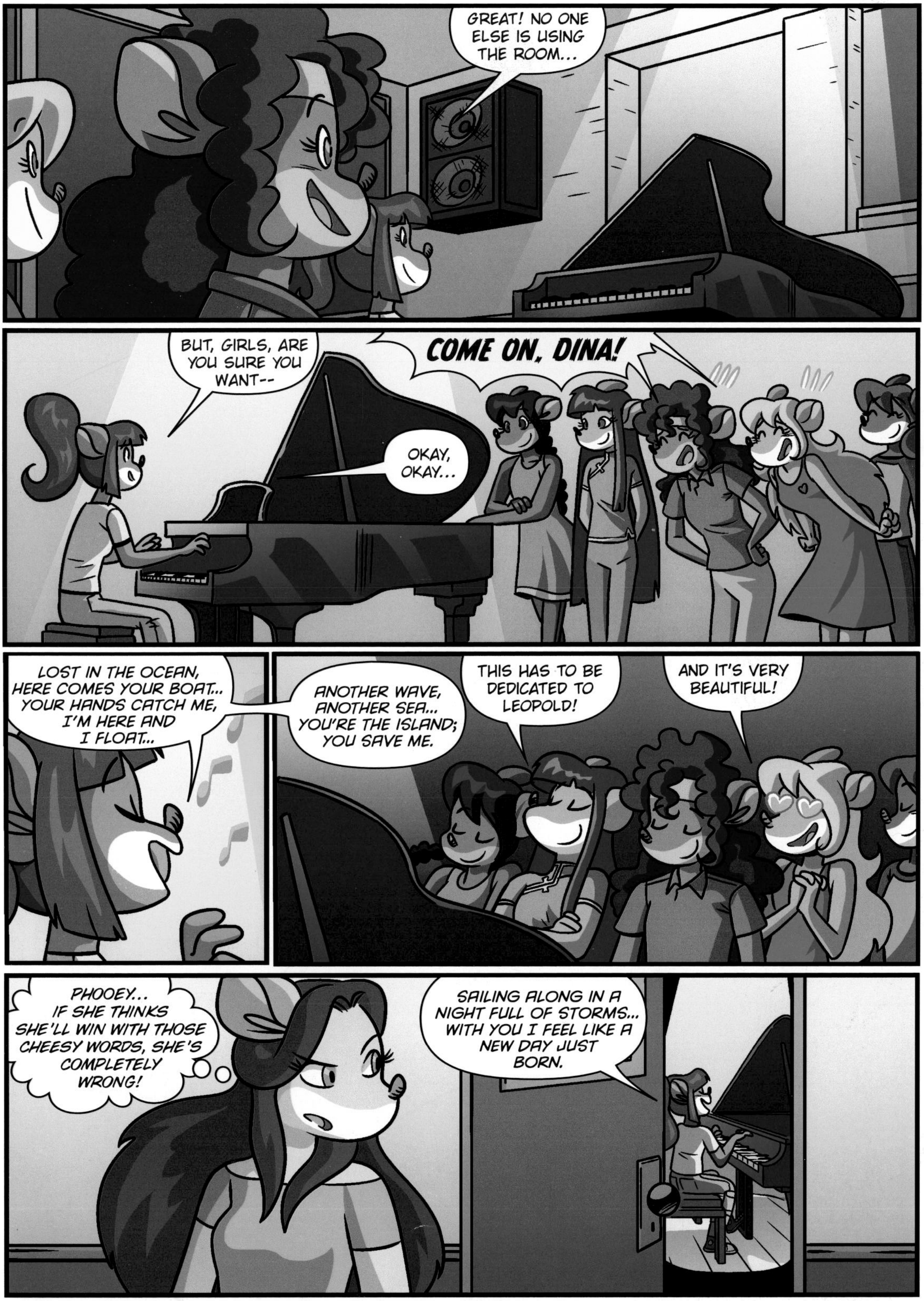
GREAT! NO ONE ELSE IS USING THE ROOM...
BUT, GIRLS, ARE YOU SURE YOU WANT--
COME ON, DINA!
OKAY, OKAY...
LOST IN THE OCEAN, HERE COMES YOUR BOAT... YOUR HANDS CATCH ME, I'M HERE AND I FLOAT...
ANOTHER WAVE, ANOTHER SEA... YOU'RE THE ISLAND; YOU SAVE ME.
THIS HAS TO BE DEDICATED TO LEOPOLD!
AND IT'S VERY BEAUTIFUL!
PHOOEY... IF SHE THINKS SHE'LL WIN WITH THOSE CHEESY WORDS, SHE'S COMPLETELY WRONG!
SAILING ALONG IN A NIGHT FULL OF STORMS... WITH YOU I FEEL LIKE A NEW DAY JUST BORN.

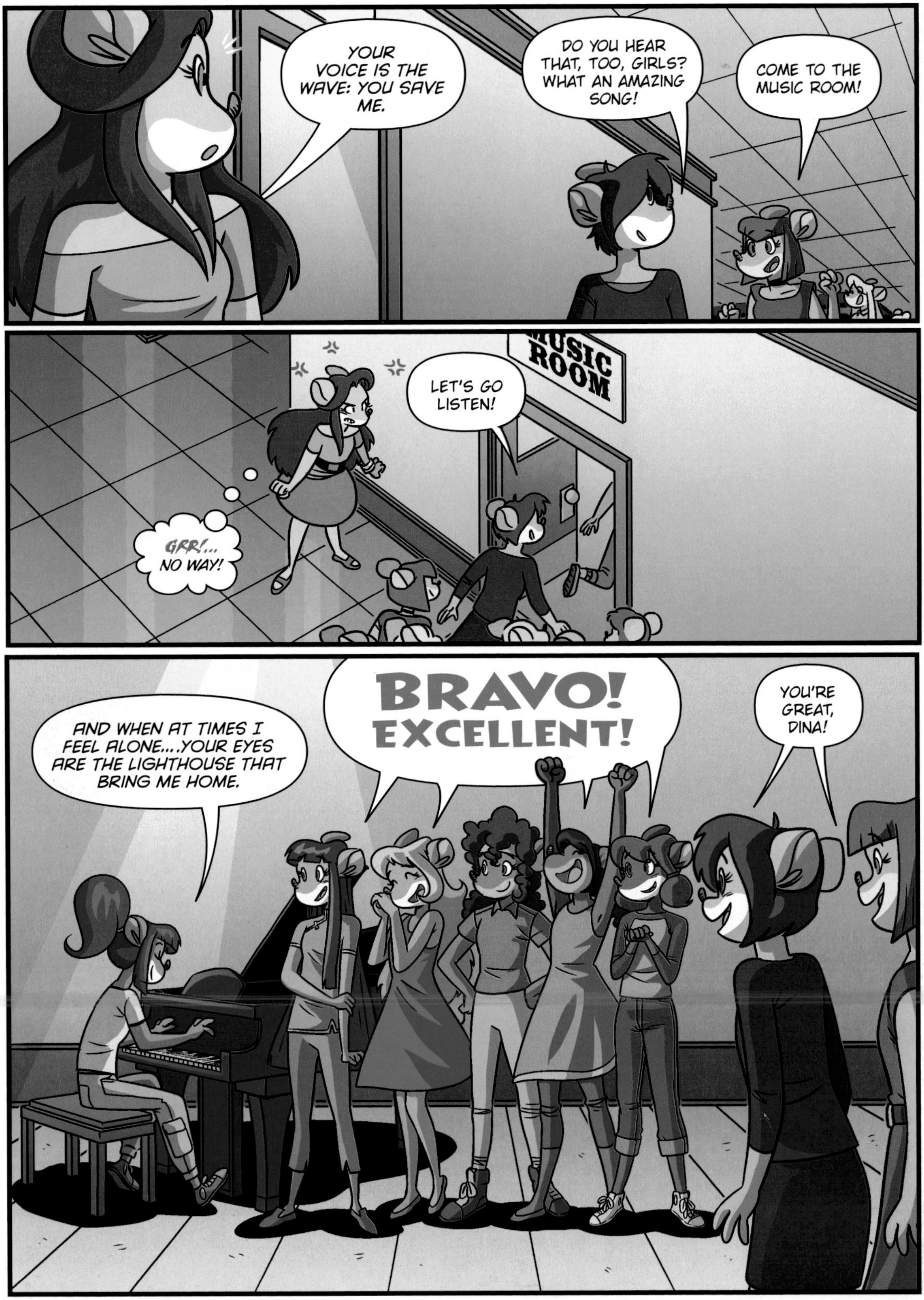
YOUR VOICE IS THE WAVE: YOU SAVE ME.
DO YOU HEAR THAT, TOO, GIRLS? WHAT AN AMAZING SONG!
COME TO THE MUSIC ROOM!
MUSIC ROOM
LET'S GO LISTEN!
GRR!... NO WAY!
AND WHEN AT TIMES I FEEL ALONE....YOUR EYES ARE THE LIGHTHOUSE THAT BRING ME HOME.
BRAVO! EXCELLENT!
YOU'RE GREAT, DINA!

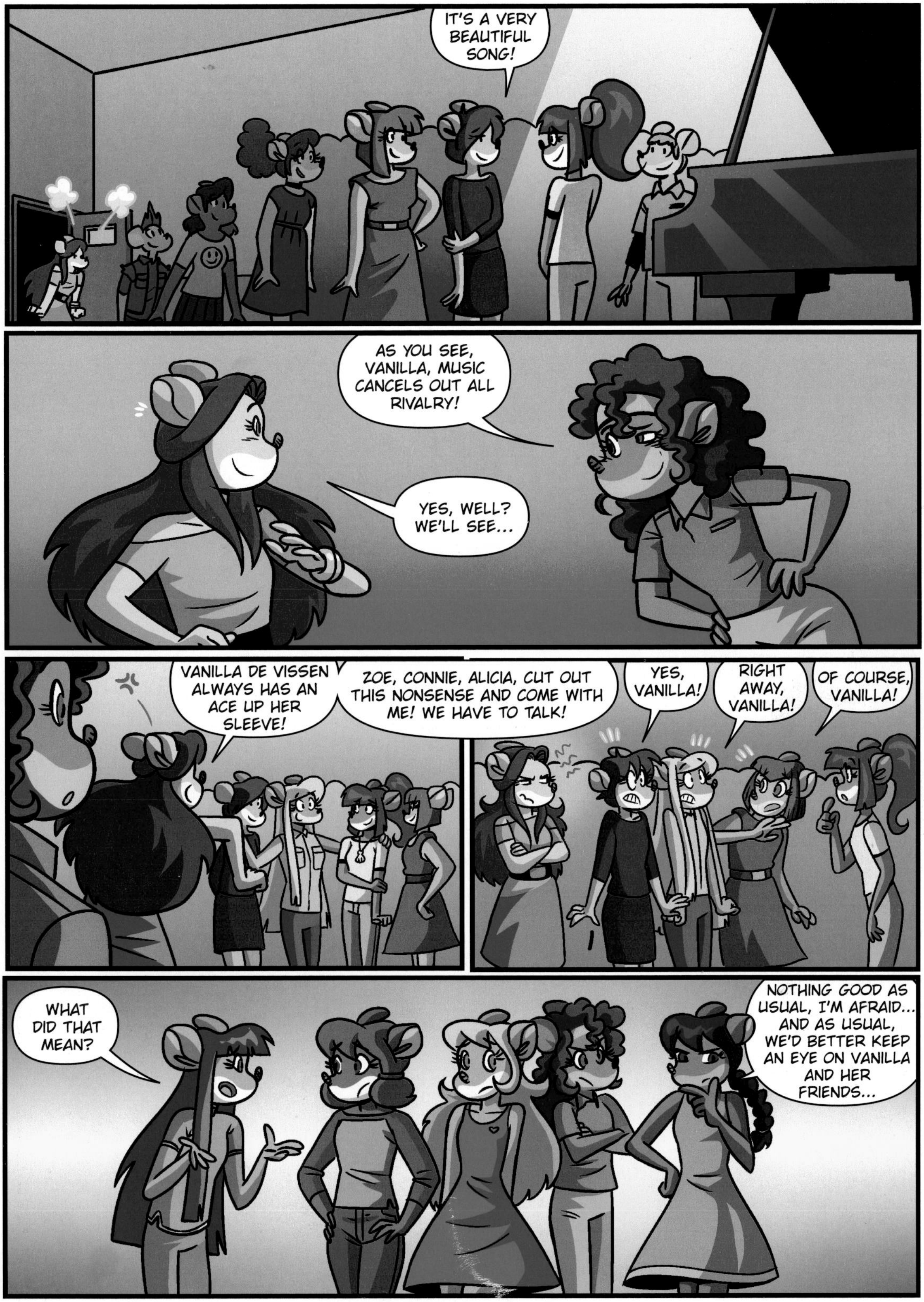

IT'S A VERY BEAUTIFUL SONG!
AS YOU SEE, VANILLA, MUSIC CANCELS OUT ALL RIVALRY!
YES, WELL? WE'LL SEE...
VANILLA DE VISSEN ALWAYS HAS AN ACE UP HER SLEEVE!
ZOE, CONNIE, ALICIA, CUT OUT THIS NONSENSE AND COME WITH ME! WE HAVE TO TALK!
YES, VANILLA!
RIGHT AWAY, VANILLA!
OF COURSE, VANILLA!
WHAT DID THAT MEAN?
NOTHING GOOD AS USUAL, I'M AFRAID... AND AS USUAL, WE'D BETTER KEEP AN EYE ON VANILLA AND HER FRIENDS...

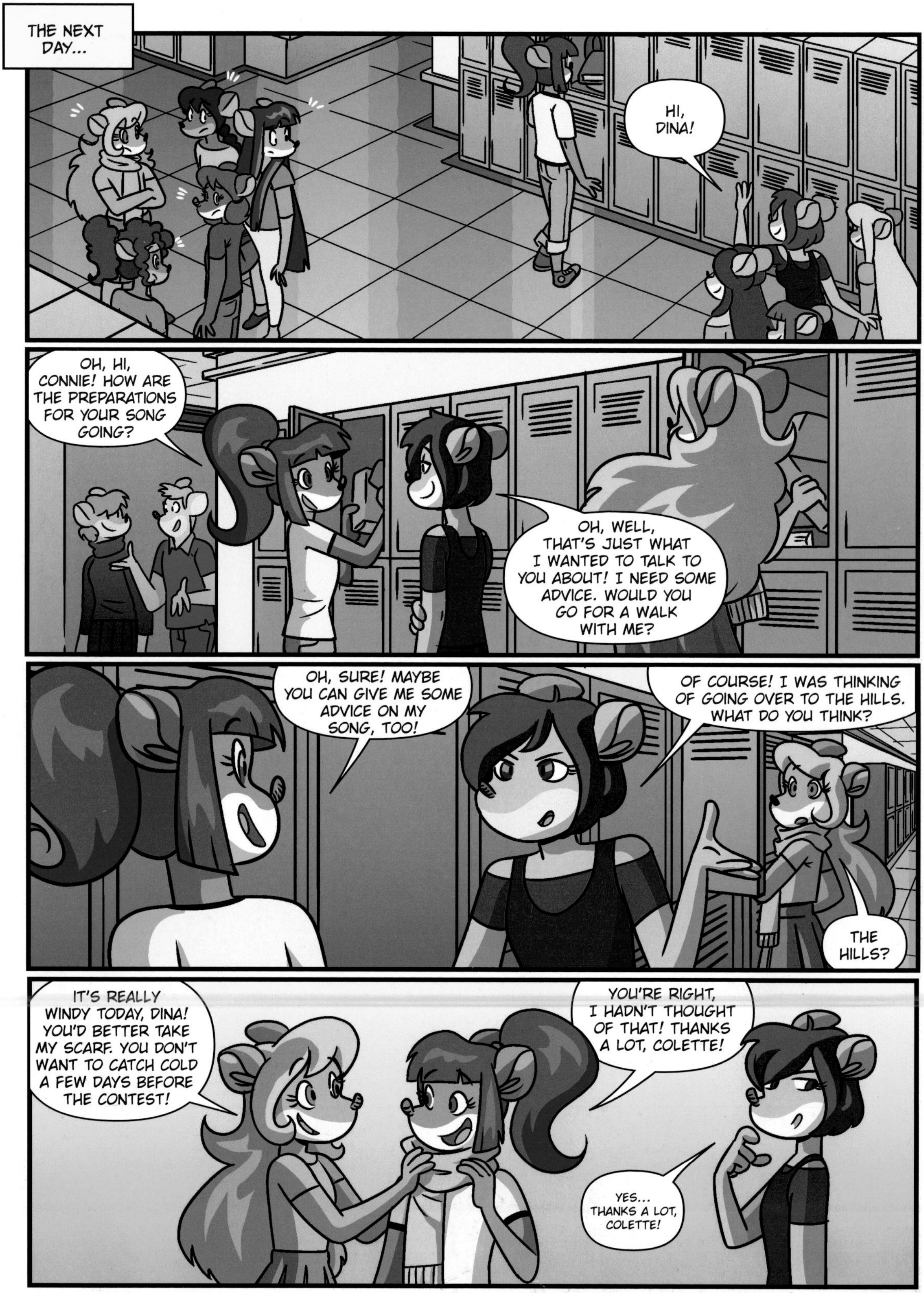
THE NEXT DAY...
HI, DINA!
OH, HI, CONNIE! HOW ARE THE PREPARATIONS FOR YOUR SONG GOING?
OH, WELL, THAT'S JUST WHAT I WANTED TO TALK TO YOU ABOUT! I NEED SOME ADVICE. WOULD YOU GO FOR A WALK WITH ME?
OH, SURE! MAYBE YOU CAN GIVE ME SOME ADVICE ON MY SONG, TOO!
OF COURSE! I WAS THINKING OF GOING OVER TO THE HILLS. WHAT DO YOU THINK?
THE HILLS?
IT'S REALLY WINDY TODAY, DINA! YOU'D BETTER TAKE MY SCARF. YOU DON'T WANT TO CATCH COLD A FEW DAYS BEFORE THE CONTEST!
YOU'RE RIGHT, I HADN'T THOUGHT OF THAT! THANKS A LOT, COLETTE!
YES... THANKS A LOT, COLETTE!

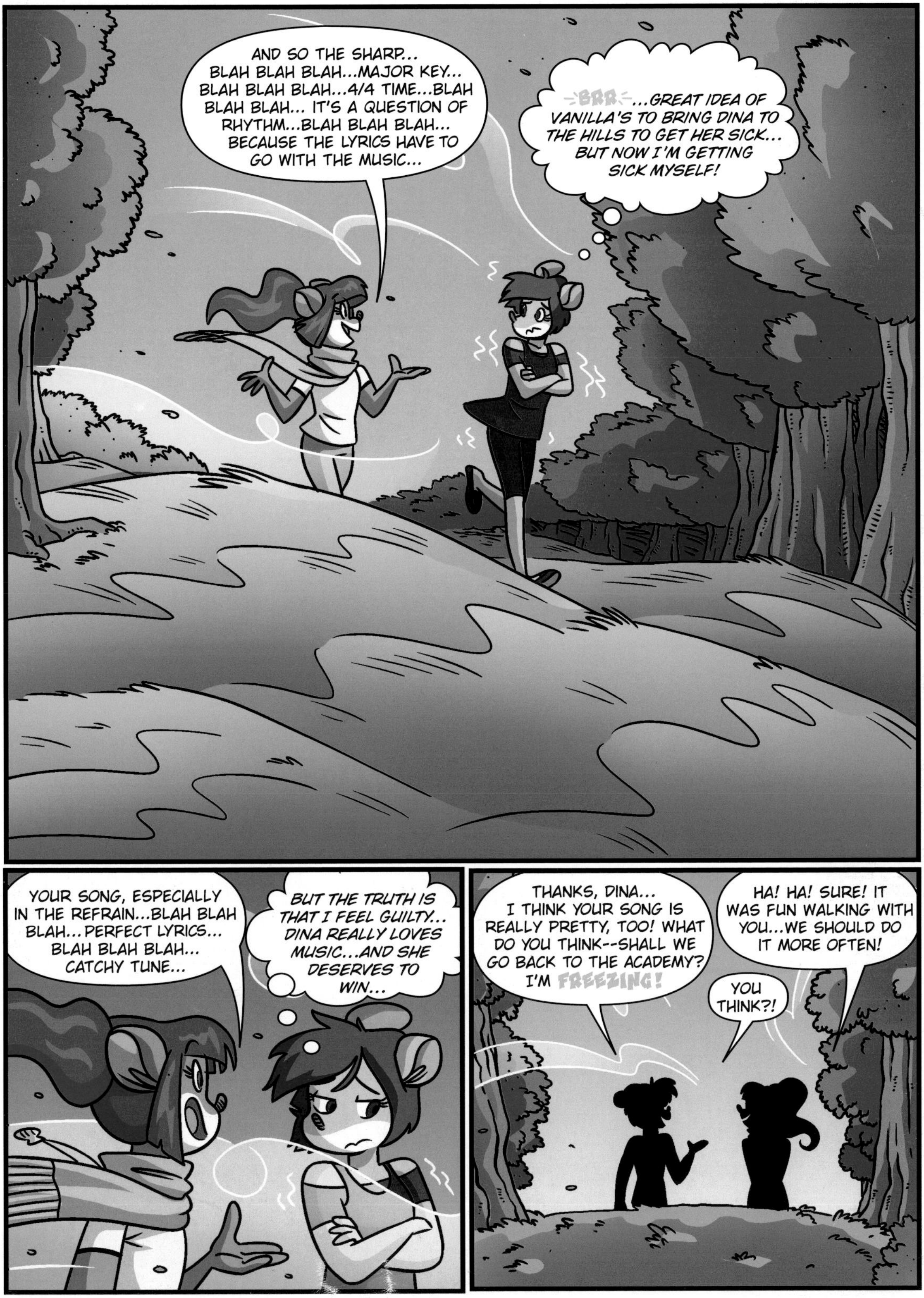
AND SO THE SHARP... BLAH BLAH BLAH...MAJOR KEY... BLAH BLAH BLAH...4/4 TIME...BLAH BLAH BLAH... IT'S A QUESTION OF RHYTHM...BLAH BLAH BLAH... BECAUSE THE LYRICS HAVE TO GO WITH THE MUSIC...
BRR...GREAT IDEA OF VANILLA'S TO BRING DINA TO THE HILLS TO GET HER SICK... BUT NOW I'M GETTING SICK MYSELF!
YOUR SONG, ESPECIALLY IN THE REFRAIN...BLAH BLAH BLAH... PERFECT LYRICS... BLAH BLAH BLAH... CATCHY TUNE...
BUT THE TRUTH IS THAT I FEEL GUILTY... DINA REALLY LOVES MUSIC...AND SHE DESERVES TO WIN...
THANKS, DINA... I THINK YOUR SONG IS REALLY PRETTY, TOO! WHAT DO YOU THINK--SHALL WE GO BACK TO THE ACADEMY? I'M FREEZING!
HA! HA! SURE! IT WAS FUN WALKING WITH YOU...WE SHOULD DO IT MORE OFTEN!
YOU THINK?!

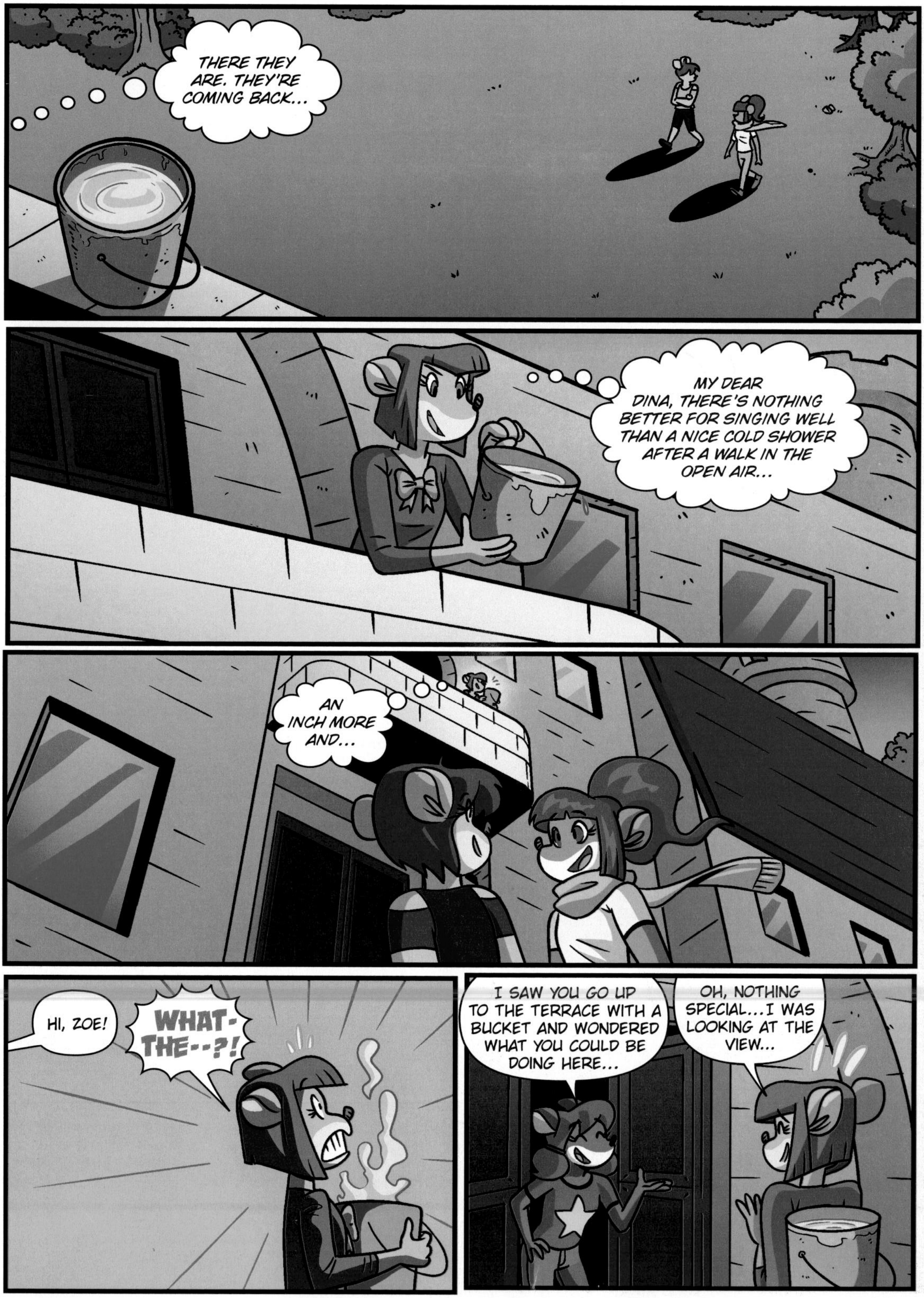

THERE THEY ARE. THEY'RE COMING BACK...
MY DEAR DINA, THERE'S NOTHING BETTER FOR SINGING WELL THAN A NICE COLD SHOWER AFTER A WALK IN THE OPEN AIR...
AN INCH MORE AND...
HI, ZOE!
WHAT-THE--?!
I SAW YOU GO UP TO THE TERRACE WITH A BUCKET AND WONDERED WHAT YOU COULD BE DOING HERE...
OH, NOTHING SPECIAL...I WAS LOOKING AT THE VIEW...

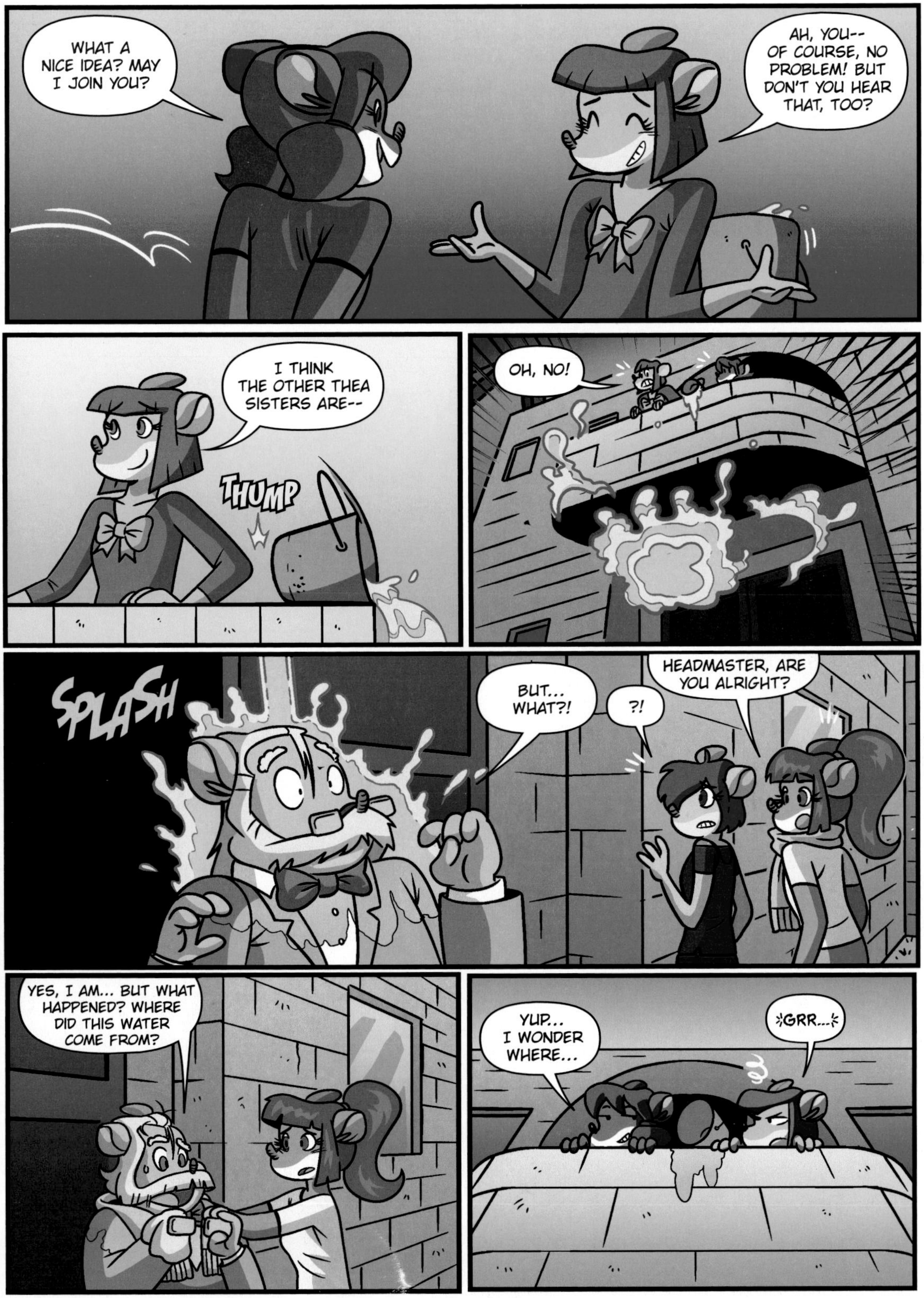

WHAT A NICE IDEA? MAY I JOIN YOU?
AH, YOU-- OF COURSE, NO PROBLEM! BUT DON'T YOU HEAR THAT, TOO?
I THINK THE OTHER THEA SISTERS ARE--
THUMP
OH, NO!
SPLASH
BUT... WHAT?!
?!
HEADMASTER, ARE YOU ALRIGHT?
YES, I AM... BUT WHAT HAPPENED? WHERE DID THIS WATER COME FROM?
YUP... I WONDER WHERE...
GRR...

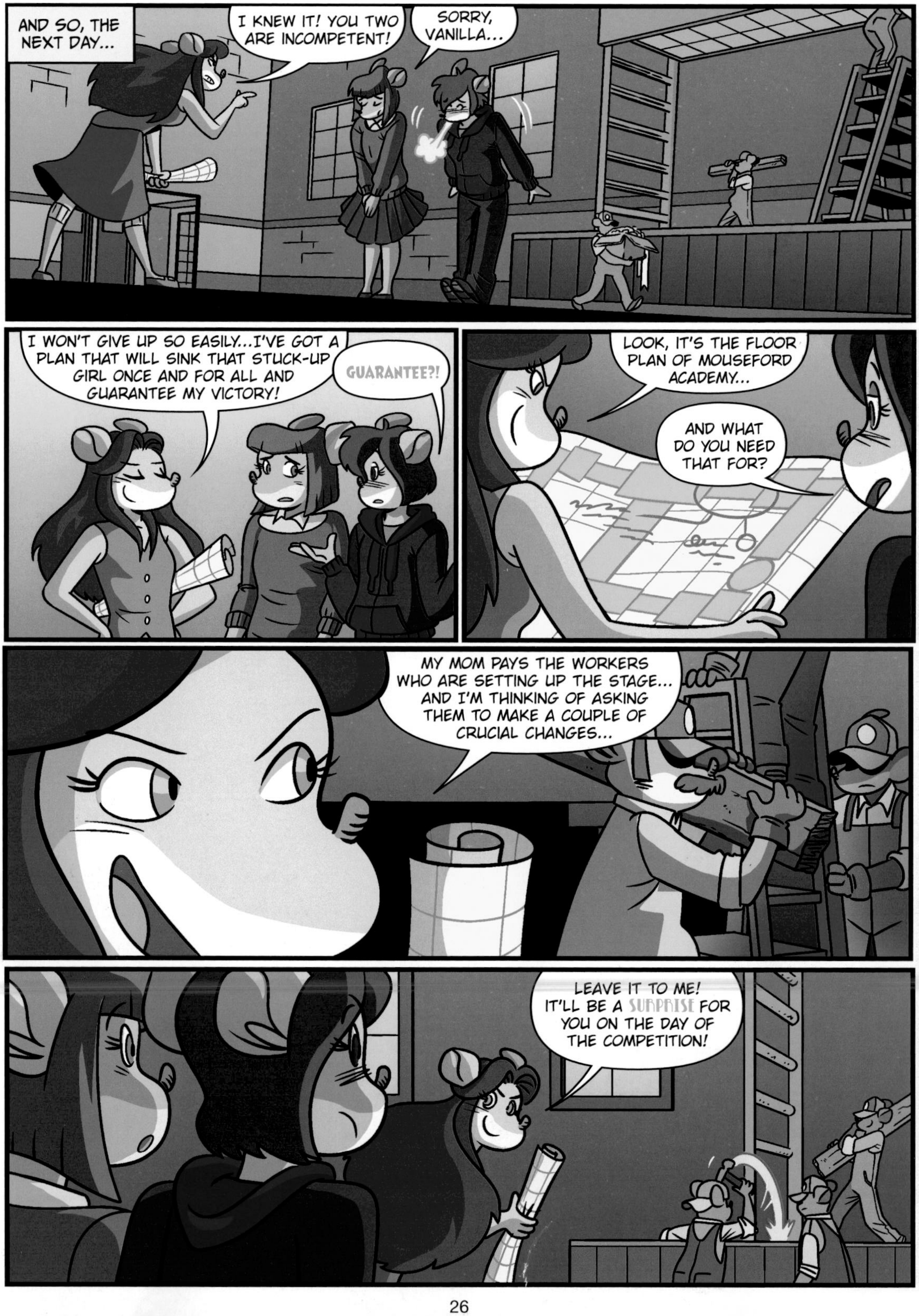
AND SO, THE NEXT DAY...
I KNEW IT! YOU TWO ARE INCOMPETENT!
SORRY, VANILLA...
I WON'T GIVE UP SO EASILY...I'VE GOT A PLAN THAT WILL SINK THAT STUCK-UP GIRL ONCE AND FOR ALL AND GUARANTEE MY VICTORY!
GUARANTEE?!
LOOK, IT'S THE FLOOR PLAN OF MOUSEFORD ACADEMY...
AND WHAT DO YOU NEED THAT FOR?
MY MOM PAYS THE WORKERS WHO ARE SETTING UP THE STAGE... AND I'M THINKING OF ASKING THEM TO MAKE A COUPLE OF CRUCIAL CHANGES...
LEAVE IT TO ME! IT'LL BE A SURPRISE FOR YOU ON THE DAY OF THE COMPETITION!

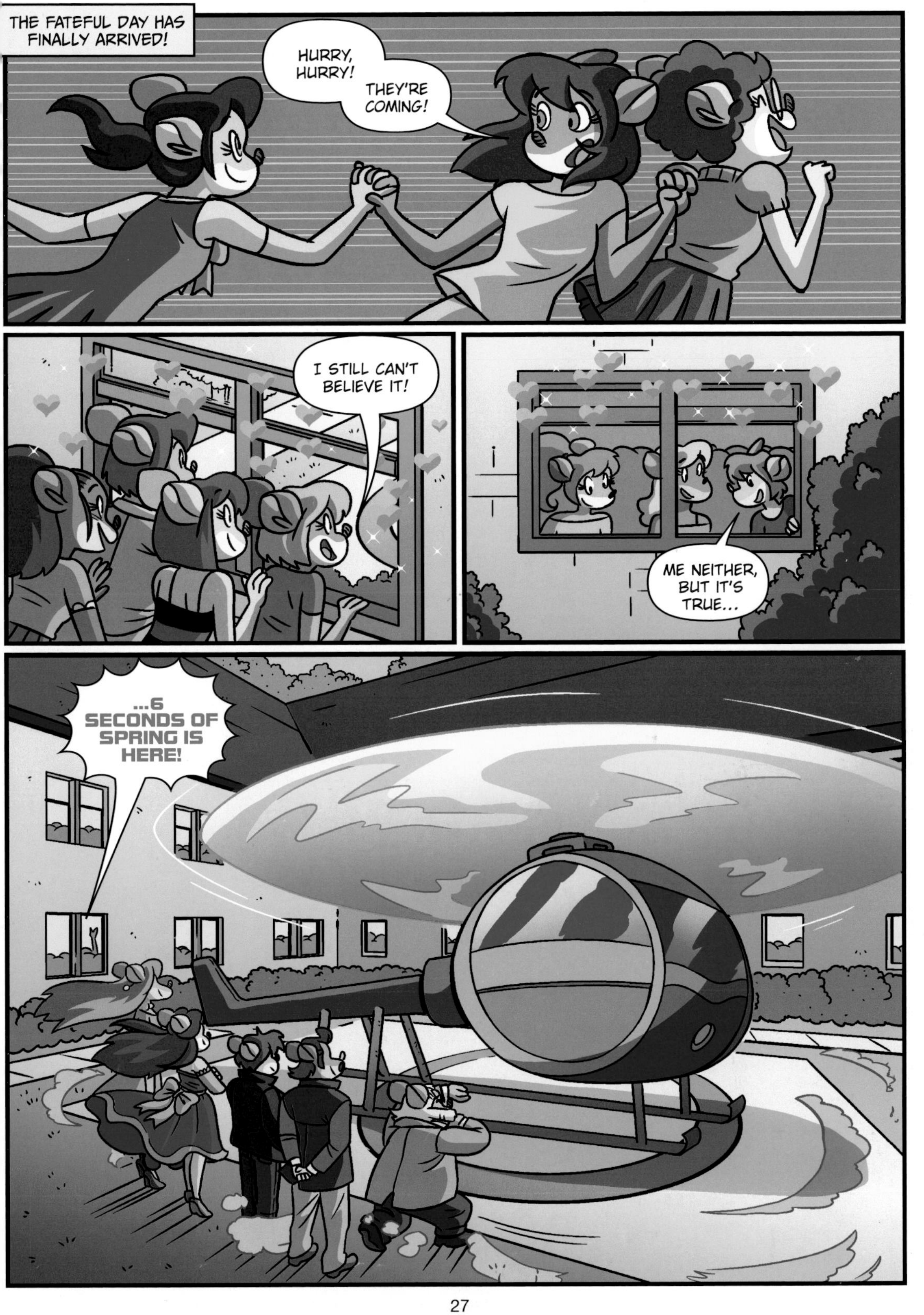
THE FATEFUL DAY HAS FINALLY ARRIVED!
HURRY, HURRY!
THEY'RE COMING!
I STILL CAN'T BELIEVE IT!
ME NEITHER, BUT IT'S TRUE...
...6 SECONDS OF SPRING IS HERE!

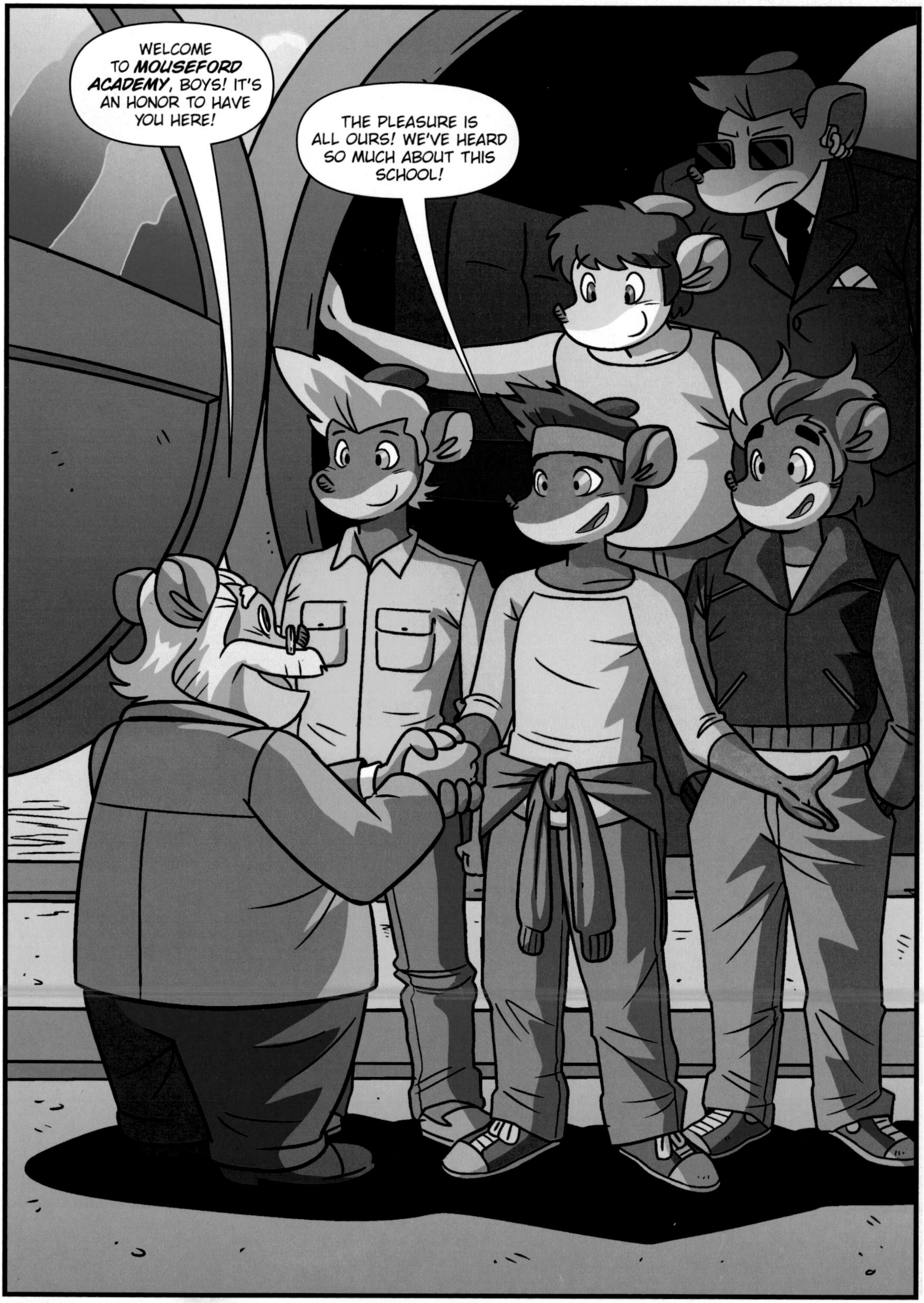
WELCOME TO **MOUSEFORD ACADEMY**, BOYS! IT'S AN HONOR TO HAVE YOU HERE!
THE PLEASURE IS ALL OURS! WE'VE HEARD SO MUCH ABOUT THIS SCHOOL!

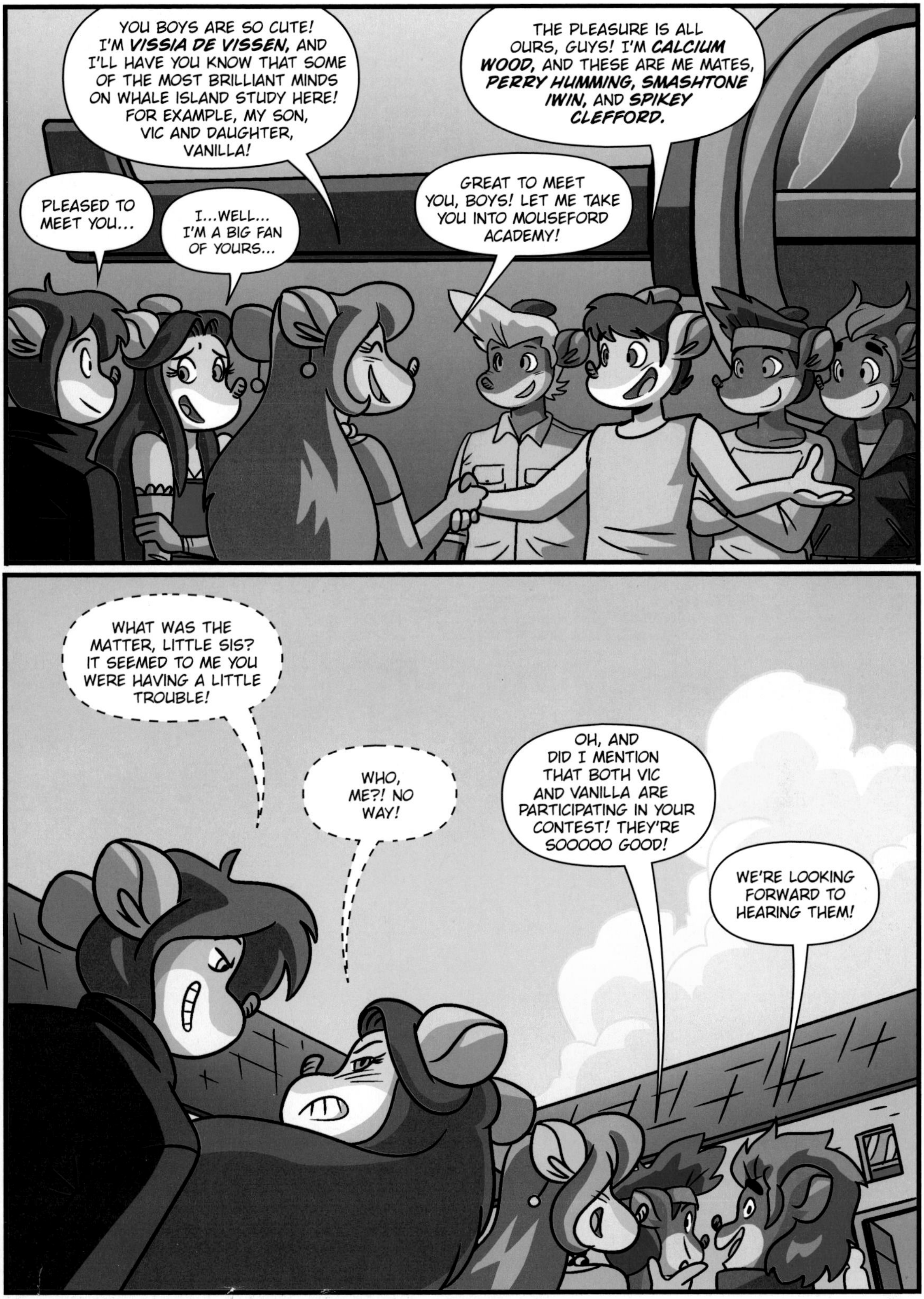
YOU BOYS ARE SO CUTE! I'M **VISSIA DE VISSEN,** AND I'LL HAVE YOU KNOW THAT SOME OF THE MOST BRILLIANT MINDS ON WHALE ISLAND STUDY HERE! FOR EXAMPLE, MY SON, VIC AND DAUGHTER, VANILLA!
PLEASED TO MEET YOU...
I...WELL... I'M A BIG FAN OF YOURS...
THE PLEASURE IS ALL OURS, GUYS! I'M **CALCIUM WOOD,** AND THESE ARE ME MATES, **PERRY HUMMING, SMASHTONE IWIN,** AND **SPIKEY CLEFFORD.**
GREAT TO MEET YOU, BOYS! LET ME TAKE YOU INTO MOUSEFORD ACADEMY!
WHAT WAS THE MATTER, LITTLE SIS? IT SEEMED TO ME YOU WERE HAVING A LITTLE TROUBLE!
WHO, ME?! NO WAY!
OH, AND DID I MENTION THAT BOTH VIC AND VANILLA ARE PARTICIPATING IN YOUR CONTEST! THEY'RE SOOOOO GOOD!
WE'RE LOOKING FORWARD TO HEARING THEM!

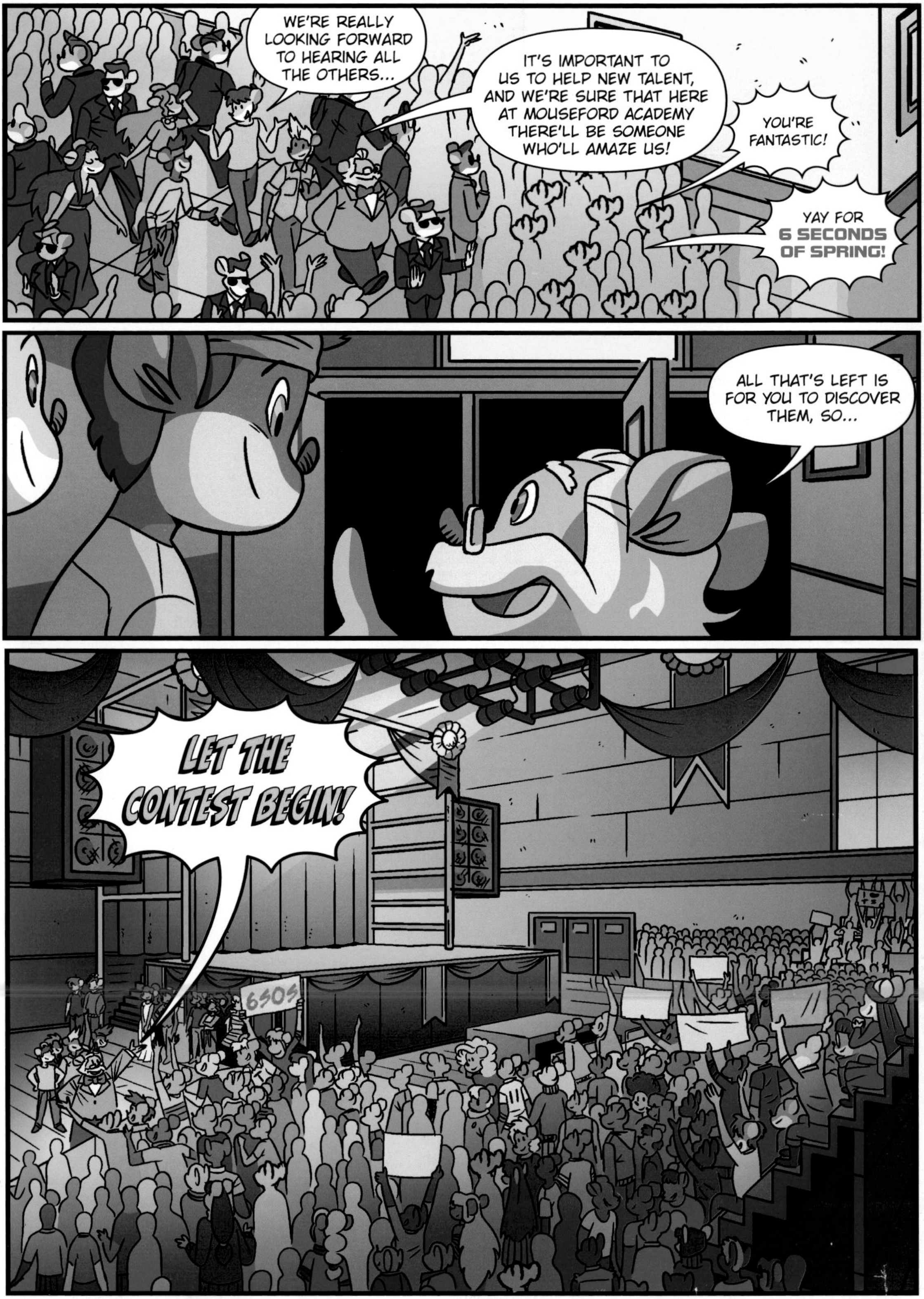
WE'RE REALLY LOOKING FORWARD TO HEARING ALL THE OTHERS...
IT'S IMPORTANT TO US TO HELP NEW TALENT, AND WE'RE SURE THAT HERE AT MOUSEFORD ACADEMY THERE'LL BE SOMEONE WHO'LL AMAZE US!
YOU'RE FANTASTIC!
YAY FOR 6 SECONDS OF SPRING!
ALL THAT'S LEFT IS FOR YOU TO DISCOVER THEM, SO...
LET THE CONTEST BEGIN!
6SOS

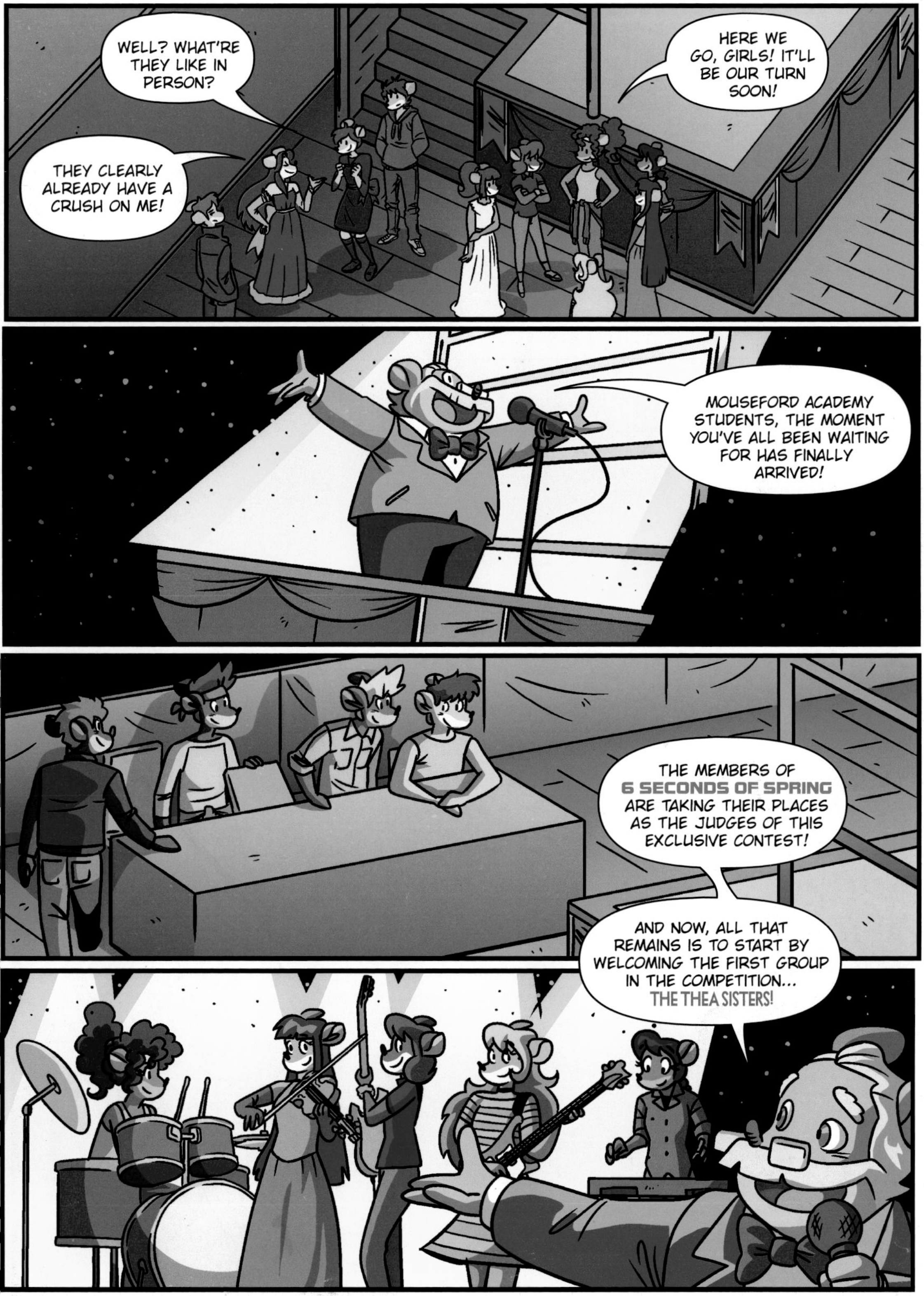
WELL? WHAT'RE THEY LIKE IN PERSON?
THEY CLEARLY ALREADY HAVE A CRUSH ON ME!
HERE WE GO, GIRLS! IT'LL BE OUR TURN SOON!
MOUSEFORD ACADEMY STUDENTS, THE MOMENT YOU'VE ALL BEEN WAITING FOR HAS FINALLY ARRIVED!
THE MEMBERS OF 6 SECONDS OF SPRING ARE TAKING THEIR PLACES AS THE JUDGES OF THIS EXCLUSIVE CONTEST!
AND NOW, ALL THAT REMAINS IS TO START BY WELCOMING THE FIRST GROUP IN THE COMPETITION... THE THEA SISTERS!

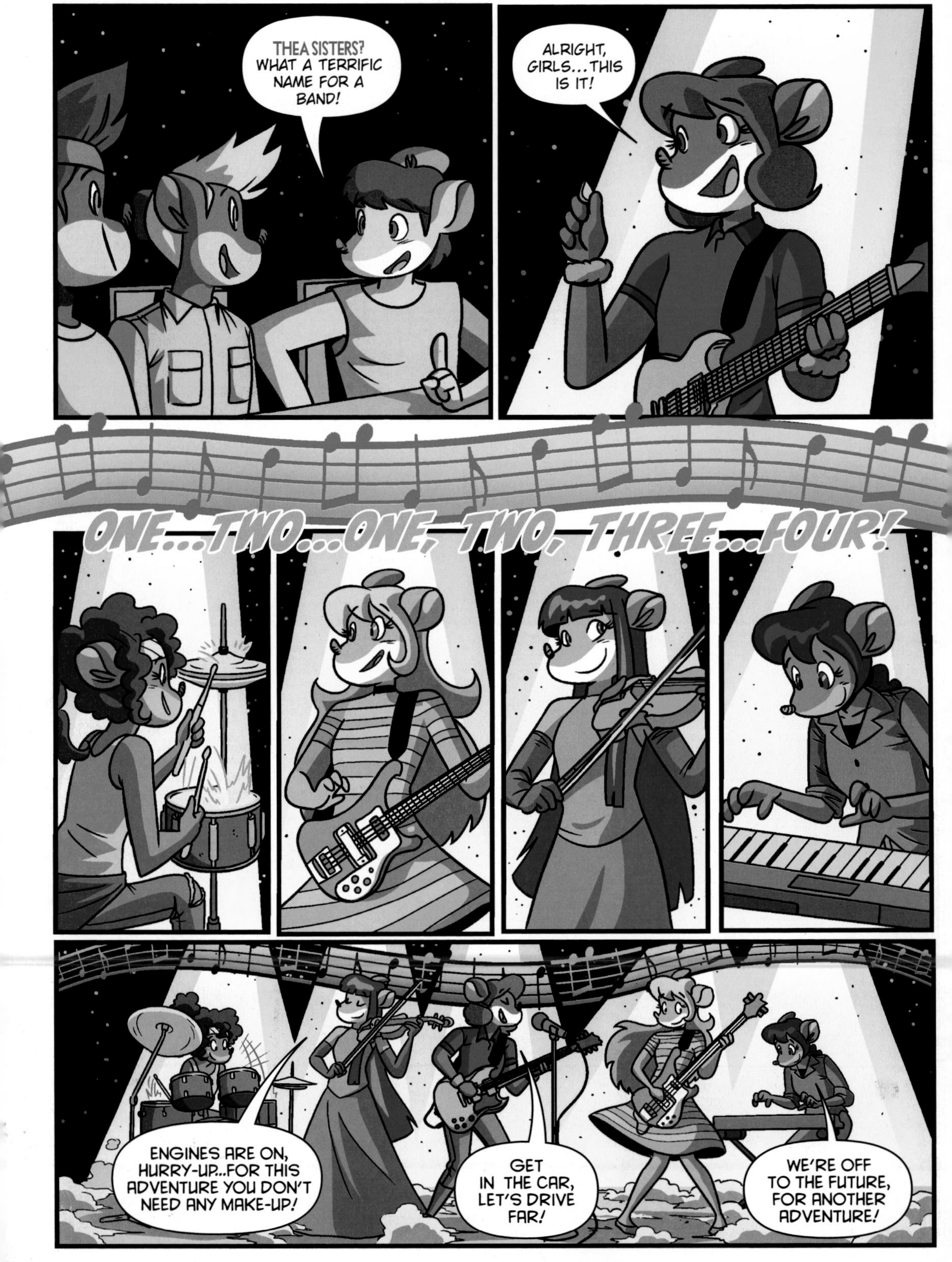

THEA SISTERS? WHAT A TERRIFIC NAME FOR A BAND!
ALRIGHT, GIRLS... THIS IS IT!
ONE... TWO... ONE, TWO, THREE... FOUR!
ENGINES ARE ON, HURRY-UP...FOR THIS ADVENTURE YOU DON'T NEED ANY MAKE-UP!
GET IN THE CAR, LET'S DRIVE FAR!
WE'RE OFF TO THE FUTURE, FOR ANOTHER ADVENTURE!

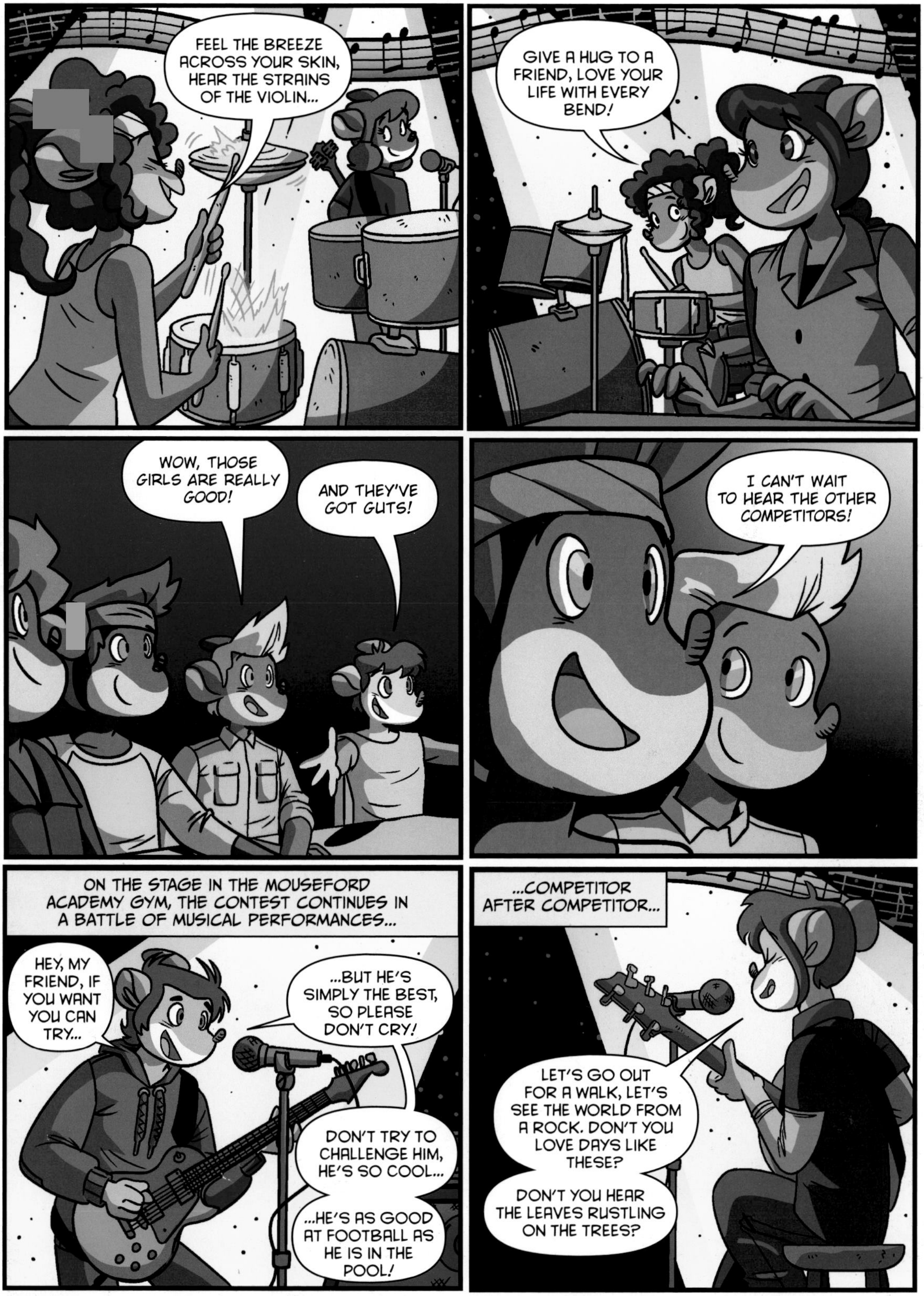
FEEL THE BREEZE ACROSS YOUR SKIN, HEAR THE STRAINS OF THE VIOLIN...
GIVE A HUG TO A FRIEND, LOVE YOUR LIFE WITH EVERY BEND!
WOW, THOSE GIRLS ARE REALLY GOOD!
AND THEY'VE GOT GUTS!
I CAN'T WAIT TO HEAR THE OTHER COMPETITORS!
ON THE STAGE IN THE MOUSEFORD ACADEMY GYM, THE CONTEST CONTINUES IN A BATTLE OF MUSICAL PERFORMANCES...
HEY, MY FRIEND, IF YOU WANT YOU CAN TRY...
...BUT HE'S SIMPLY THE BEST, SO PLEASE DON'T CRY!
DON'T TRY TO CHALLENGE HIM, HE'S SO COOL...
...HE'S AS GOOD AT FOOTBALL AS HE IS IN THE POOL!
...COMPETITOR AFTER COMPETITOR...
LET'S GO OUT FOR A WALK, LET'S SEE THE WORLD FROM A ROCK. DON'T YOU LOVE DAYS LIKE THESE?
DON'T YOU HEAR THE LEAVES RUSTLING ON THE TREES?

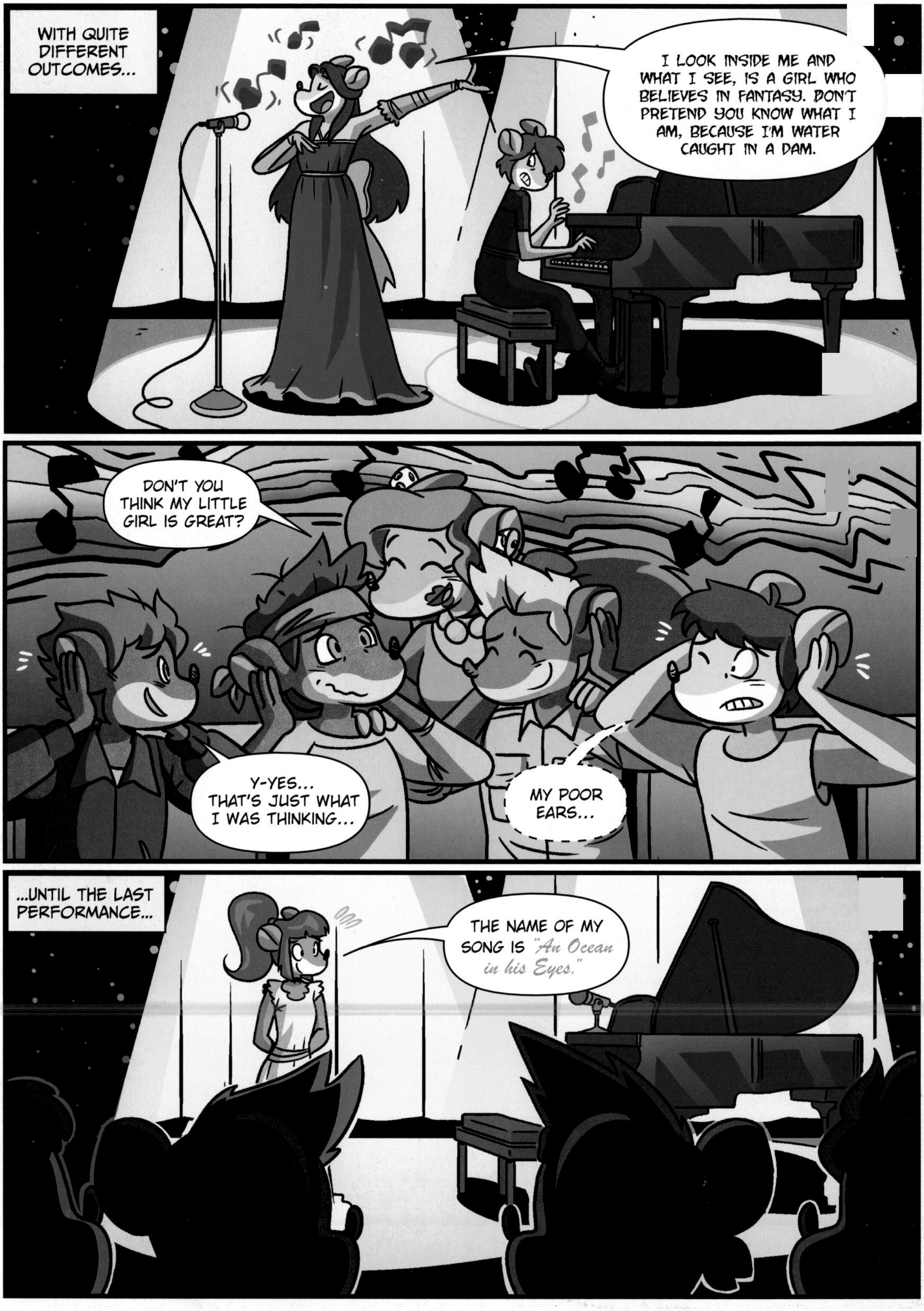
WITH QUITE DIFFERENT OUTCOMES...
I LOOK INSIDE ME AND WHAT I SEE, IS A GIRL WHO BELIEVES IN FANTASY. DON'T PRETEND YOU KNOW WHAT I AM, BECAUSE I'M WATER CAUGHT IN A DAM.
DON'T YOU THINK MY LITTLE GIRL IS GREAT?
Y-YES... THAT'S JUST WHAT I WAS THINKING...
MY POOR EARS...
...UNTIL THE LAST PERFORMANCE...
THE NAME OF MY SONG IS "An Ocean in his Eyes."

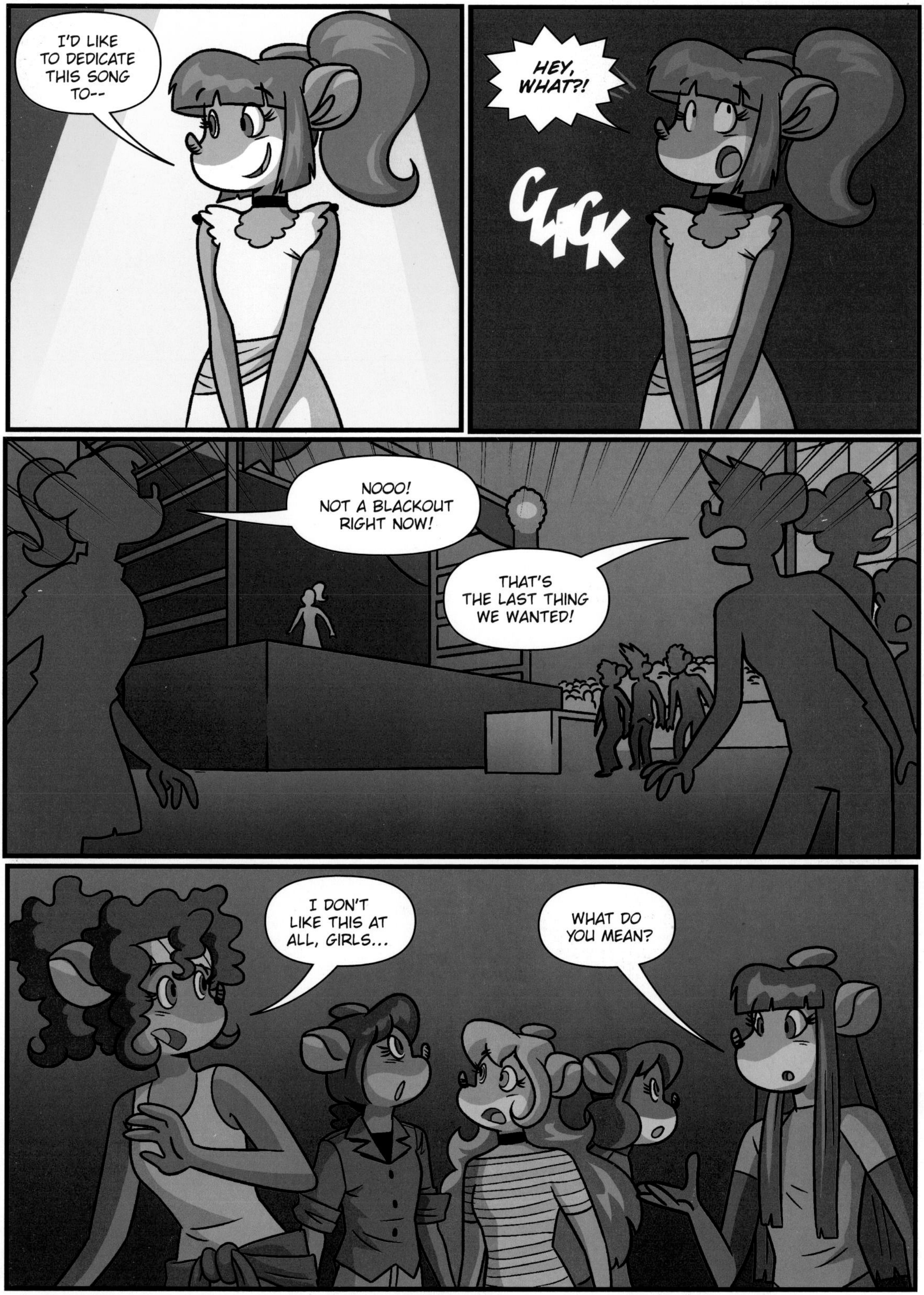
I'D LIKE TO DEDICATE THIS SONG TO--
HEY, WHAT?!
CLICK
NOOO! NOT A BLACKOUT RIGHT NOW!
THAT'S THE LAST THING WE WANTED!
I DON'T LIKE THIS AT ALL, GIRLS...
WHAT DO YOU MEAN?

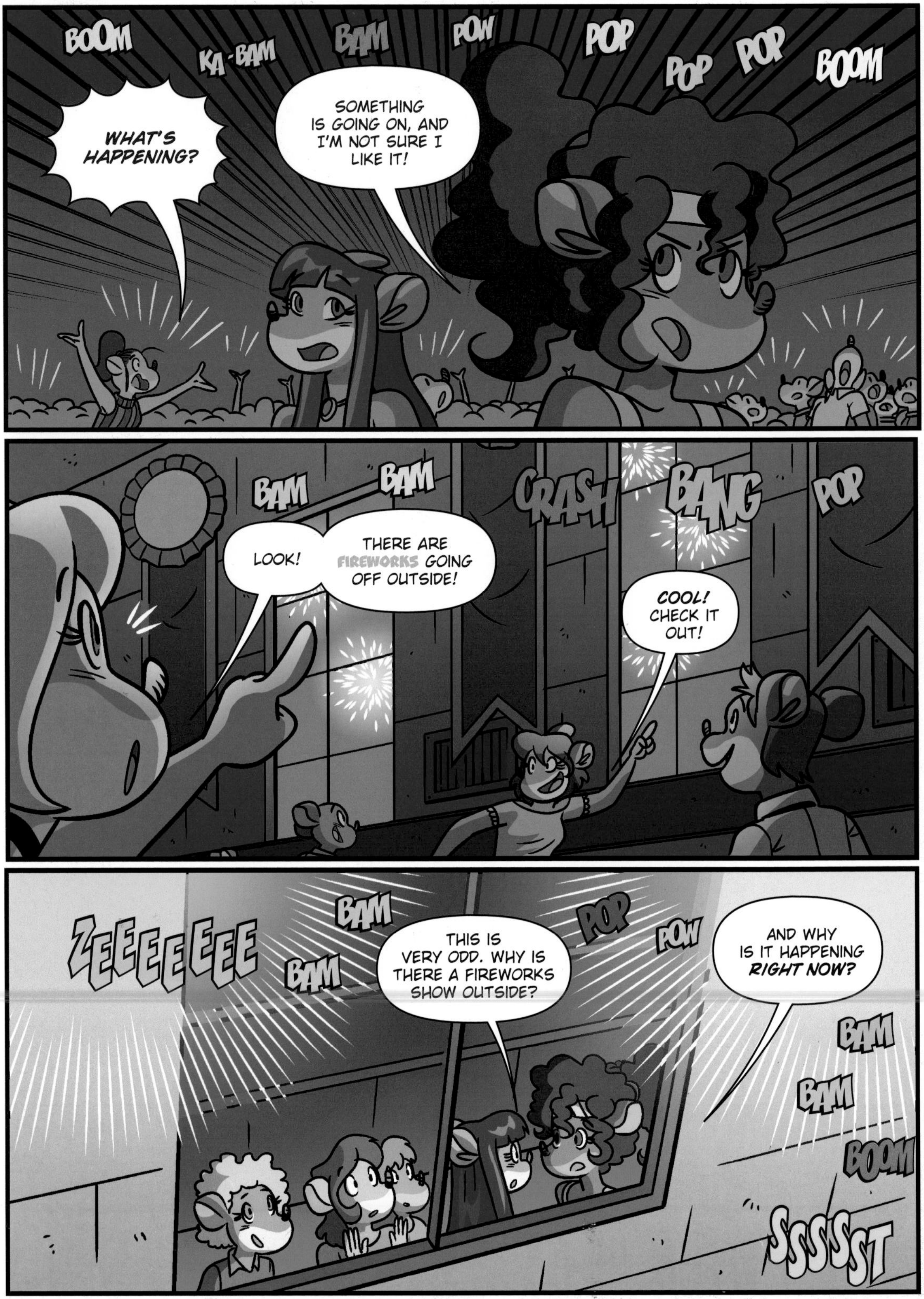
BOOM
KA-BAM
BAM
POW
POP
POP
POP
BOOM
WHAT'S HAPPENING?
SOMETHING IS GOING ON, AND I'M NOT SURE I LIKE IT!
BAM
BAM
CRASH
BANG
POP
LOOK!
THERE ARE FIREWORKS GOING OFF OUTSIDE!
COOL! CHECK IT OUT!
ZEEEEEEE
BAM
BAM
POP
POW
THIS IS VERY ODD. WHY IS THERE A FIREWORKS SHOW OUTSIDE?
AND WHY IS IT HAPPENING RIGHT NOW?
BAM
BAM
BOOM
SSSSST

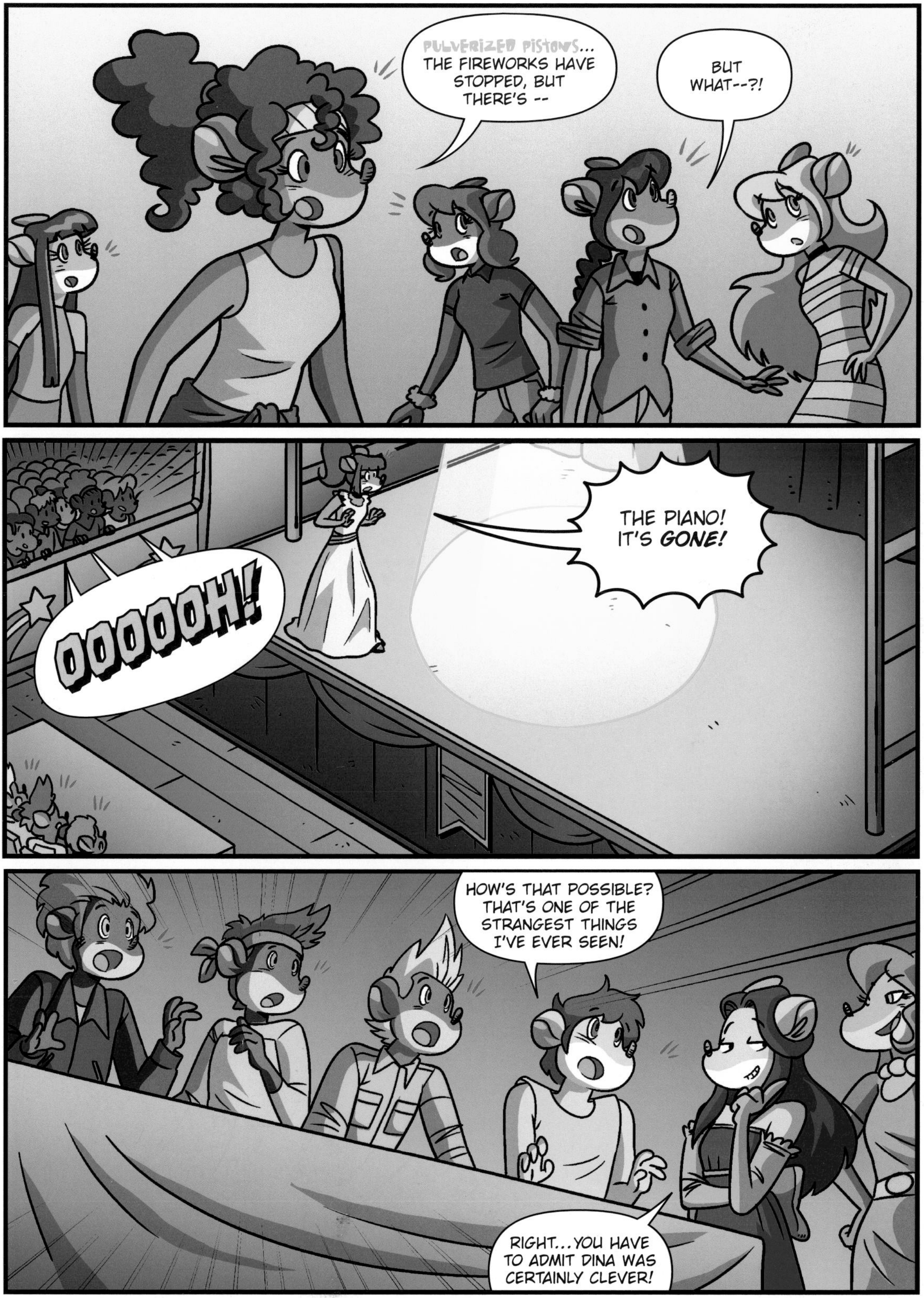
PULVERIZED PISTONS... THE FIREWORKS HAVE STOPPED, BUT THERE'S --
BUT WHAT--?!
THE PIANO! IT'S **GONE!**
OOOOOH!
HOW'S THAT POSSIBLE? THAT'S ONE OF THE STRANGEST THINGS I'VE EVER SEEN!
RIGHT... YOU HAVE TO ADMIT DINA WAS CERTAINLY CLEVER!

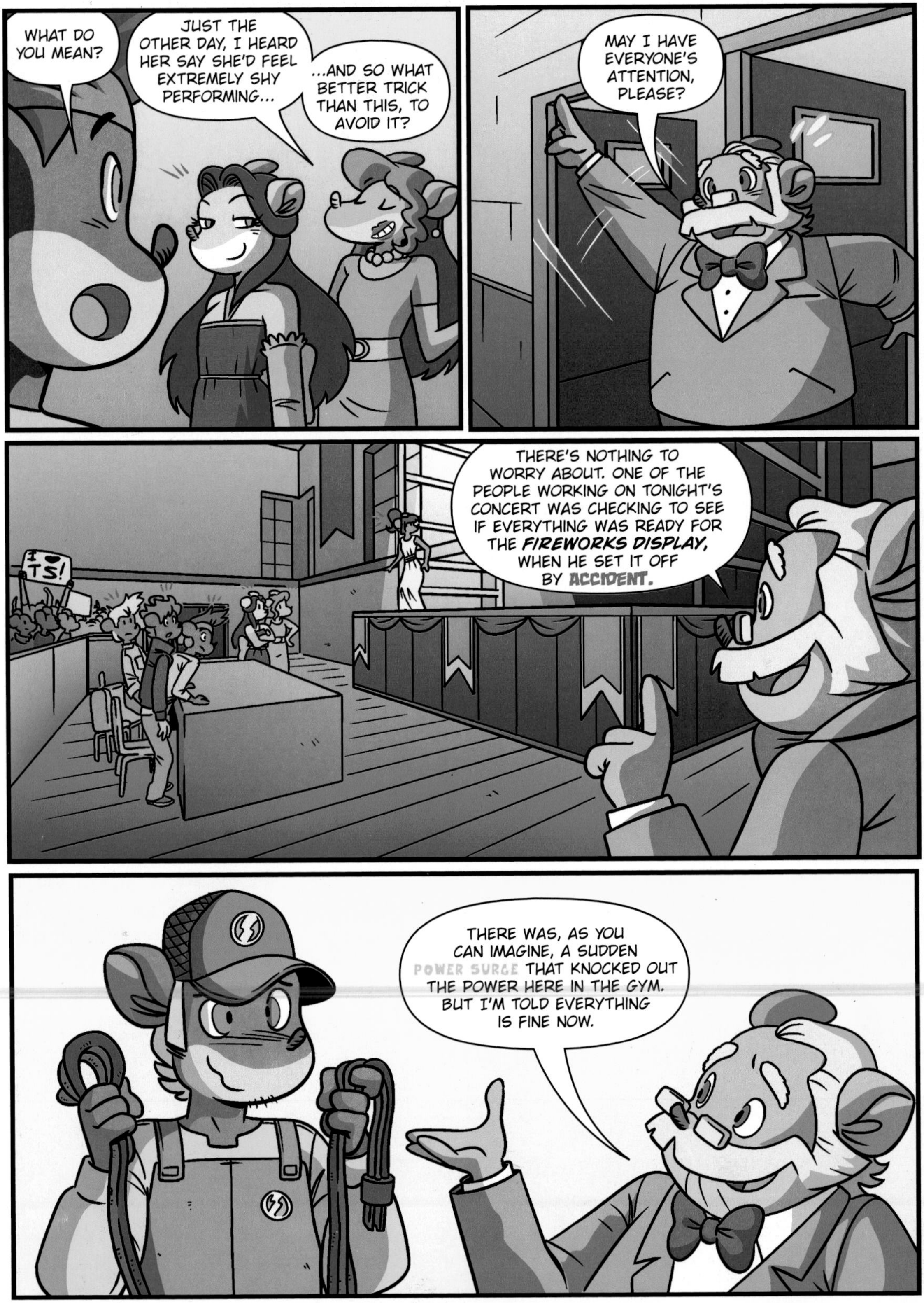
WHAT DO YOU MEAN?
JUST THE OTHER DAY, I HEARD HER SAY SHE'D FEEL EXTREMELY SHY PERFORMING...
...AND SO WHAT BETTER TRICK THAN THIS, TO AVOID IT?
MAY I HAVE EVERYONE'S ATTENTION, PLEASE?
I ♥ TS!
THERE'S NOTHING TO WORRY ABOUT. ONE OF THE PEOPLE WORKING ON TONIGHT'S CONCERT WAS CHECKING TO SEE IF EVERYTHING WAS READY FOR THE FIREWORKS DISPLAY, WHEN HE SET IT OFF BY ACCIDENT.
THERE WAS, AS YOU CAN IMAGINE, A SUDDEN POWER SURGE THAT KNOCKED OUT THE POWER HERE IN THE GYM. BUT I'M TOLD EVERYTHING IS FINE NOW.

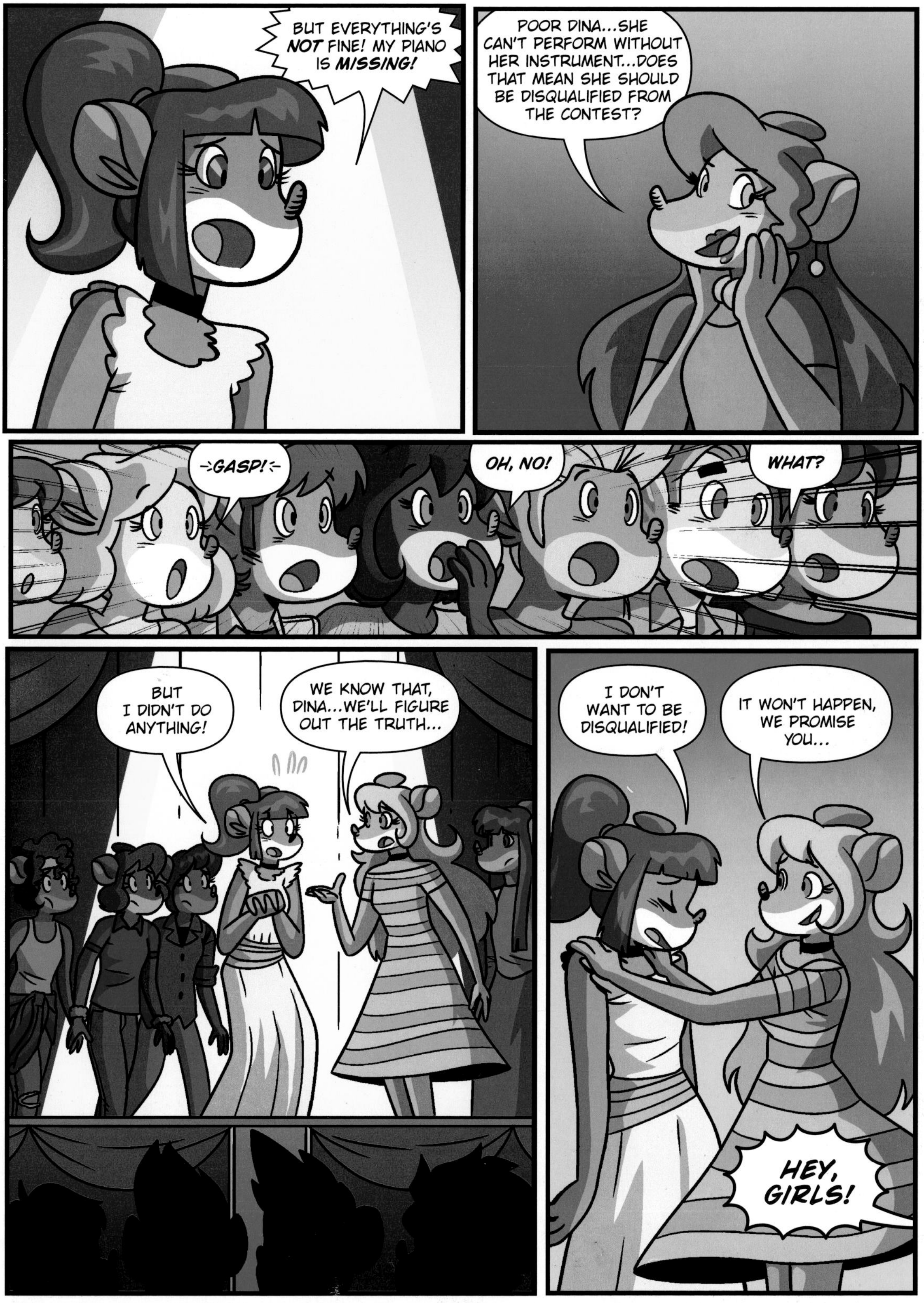
BUT EVERYTHING'S **NOT** FINE! MY PIANO IS ***MISSING!***
POOR DINA...SHE CAN'T PERFORM WITHOUT HER INSTRUMENT...DOES THAT MEAN SHE SHOULD BE DISQUALIFIED FROM THE CONTEST?
GASP!
OH, NO!
WHAT?
BUT I DIDN'T DO ANYTHING!
WE KNOW THAT, DINA...WE'LL FIGURE OUT THE TRUTH...
I DON'T WANT TO BE DISQUALIFIED!
IT WON'T HAPPEN, WE PROMISE YOU...
HEY, GIRLS!

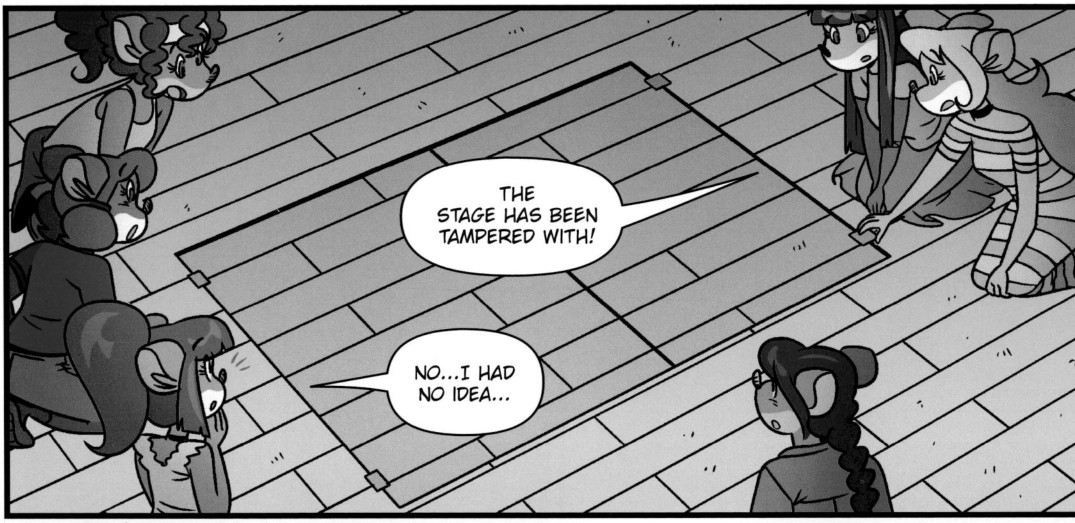
THE STAGE HAS BEEN TAMPERED WITH!
NO...I HAD NO IDEA...

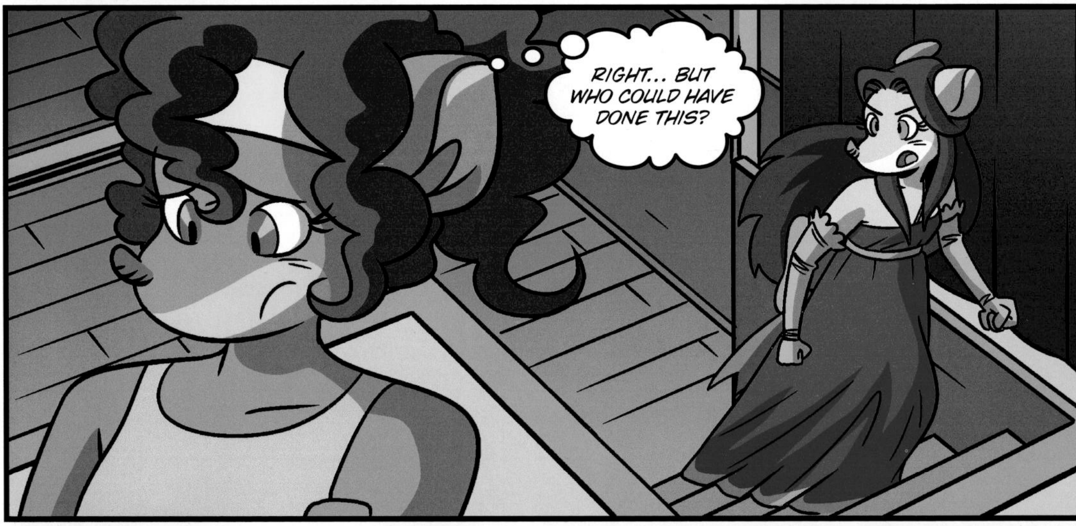
RIGHT... BUT WHO COULD HAVE DONE THIS?

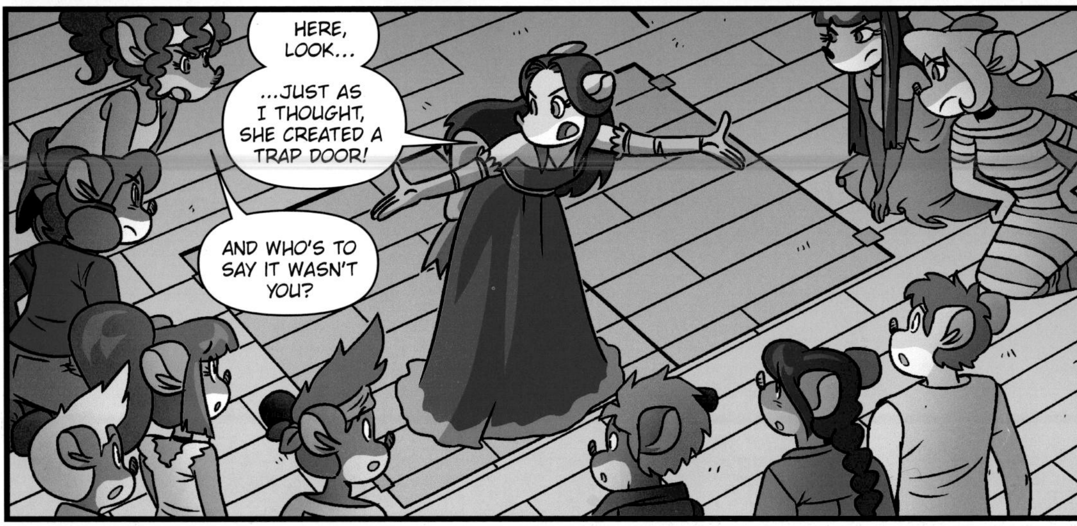
HERE, LOOK...
...JUST AS I THOUGHT, SHE CREATED A TRAP DOOR!
AND WHO'S TO SAY IT WASN'T YOU?

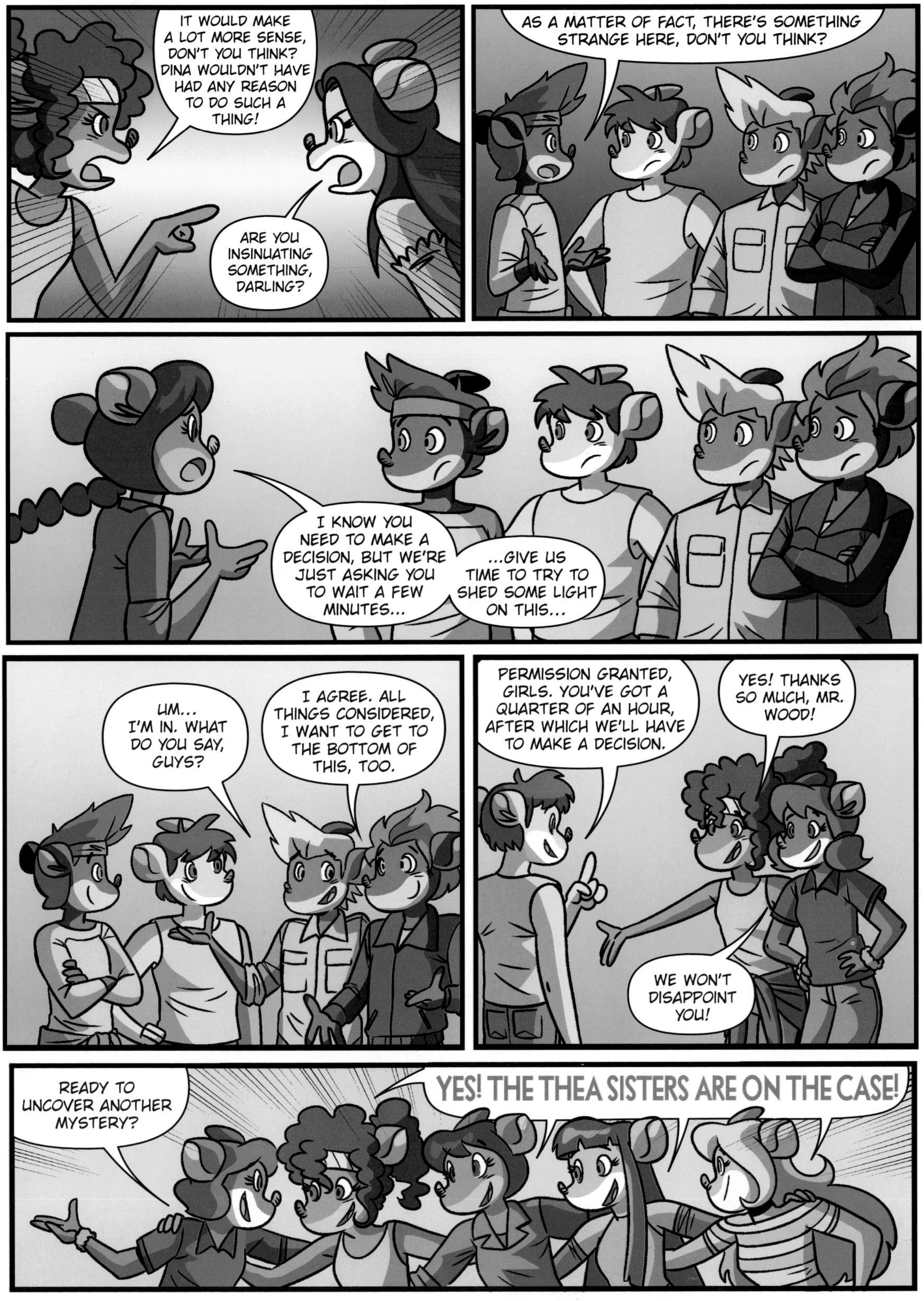
IT WOULD MAKE A LOT MORE SENSE, DON'T YOU THINK? DINA WOULDN'T HAVE HAD ANY REASON TO DO SUCH A THING!
ARE YOU INSINUATING SOMETHING, DARLING?
AS A MATTER OF FACT, THERE'S SOMETHING STRANGE HERE, DON'T YOU THINK?
I KNOW YOU NEED TO MAKE A DECISION, BUT WE'RE JUST ASKING YOU TO WAIT A FEW MINUTES...
...GIVE US TIME TO TRY TO SHED SOME LIGHT ON THIS...
UM... I'M IN. WHAT DO YOU SAY, GUYS?
I AGREE. ALL THINGS CONSIDERED, I WANT TO GET TO THE BOTTOM OF THIS, TOO.
PERMISSION GRANTED, GIRLS. YOU'VE GOT A QUARTER OF AN HOUR, AFTER WHICH WE'LL HAVE TO MAKE A DECISION.
YES! THANKS SO MUCH, MR. WOOD!
WE WON'T DISAPPOINT YOU!
READY TO UNCOVER ANOTHER MYSTERY?
YES! THE THEA SISTERS ARE ON THE CASE!

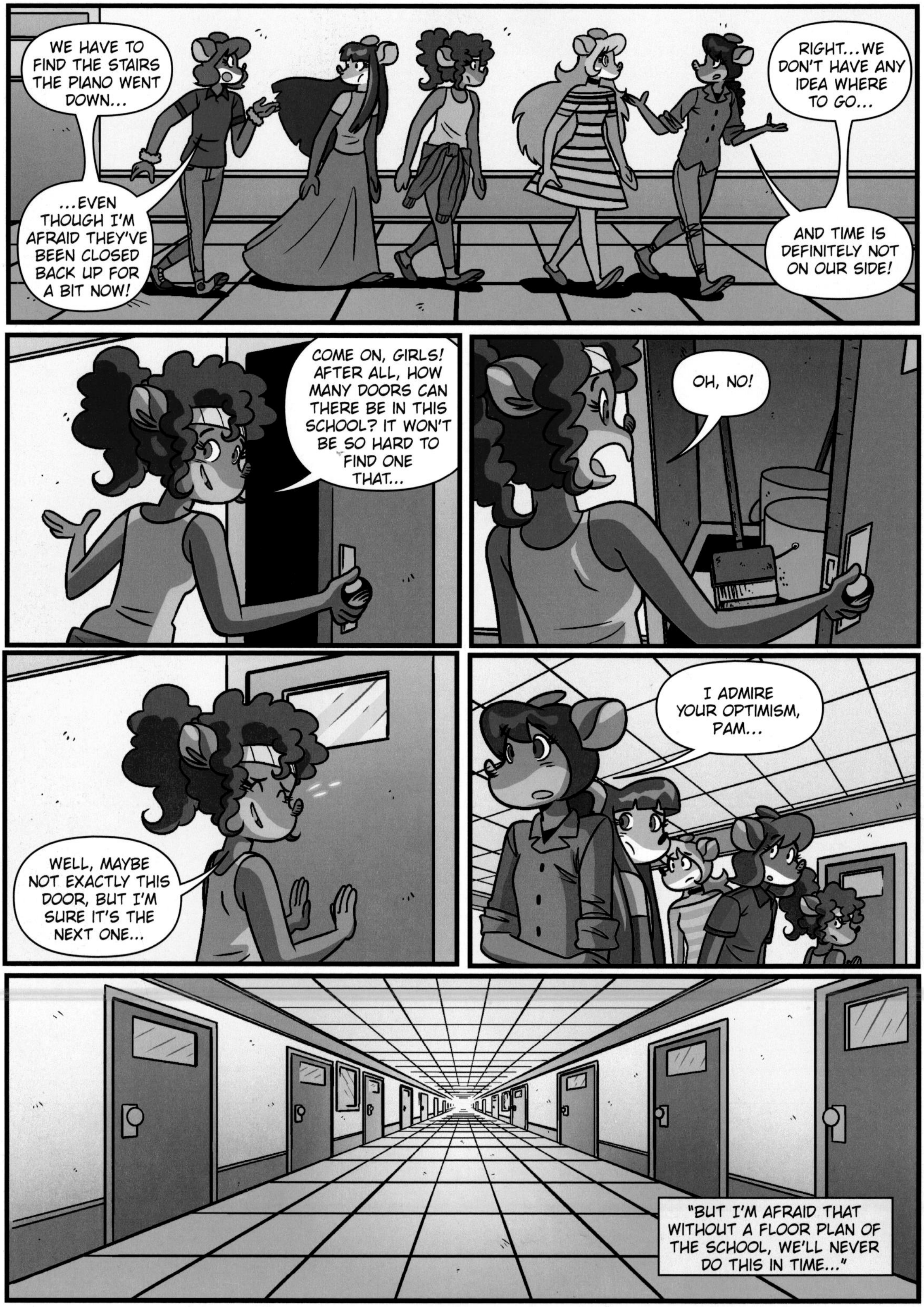
WE HAVE TO FIND THE STAIRS THE PIANO WENT DOWN...
...EVEN THOUGH I'M AFRAID THEY'VE BEEN CLOSED BACK UP FOR A BIT NOW!
RIGHT...WE DON'T HAVE ANY IDEA WHERE TO GO...
AND TIME IS DEFINITELY NOT ON OUR SIDE!
COME ON, GIRLS! AFTER ALL, HOW MANY DOORS CAN THERE BE IN THIS SCHOOL? IT WON'T BE SO HARD TO FIND ONE THAT...
OH, NO!
WELL, MAYBE NOT EXACTLY THIS DOOR, BUT I'M SURE IT'S THE NEXT ONE...
I ADMIRE YOUR OPTIMISM, PAM...
"BUT I'M AFRAID THAT WITHOUT A FLOOR PLAN OF THE SCHOOL, WE'LL NEVER DO THIS IN TIME..."

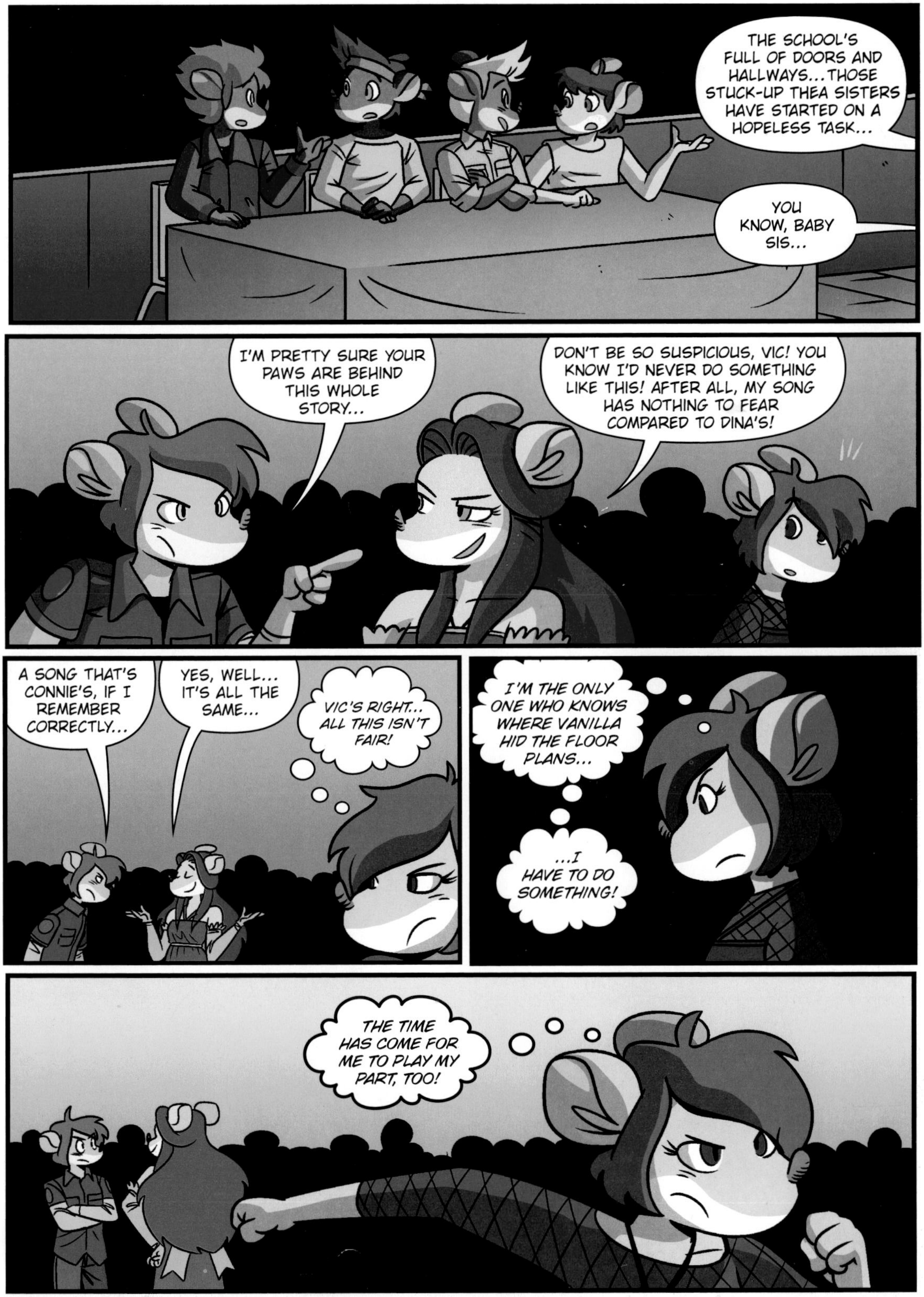
THE SCHOOL'S FULL OF DOORS AND HALLWAYS...THOSE STUCK-UP THEA SISTERS HAVE STARTED ON A HOPELESS TASK...
YOU KNOW, BABY SIS...
I'M PRETTY SURE YOUR PAWS ARE BEHIND THIS WHOLE STORY...
DON'T BE SO SUSPICIOUS, VIC! YOU KNOW I'D NEVER DO SOMETHING LIKE THIS! AFTER ALL, MY SONG HAS NOTHING TO FEAR COMPARED TO DINA'S!
A SONG THAT'S CONNIE'S, IF I REMEMBER CORRECTLY...
YES, WELL... IT'S ALL THE SAME...
VIC'S RIGHT... ALL THIS ISN'T FAIR!
I'M THE ONLY ONE WHO KNOWS WHERE VANILLA HID THE FLOOR PLANS...
...I HAVE TO DO SOMETHING!
THE TIME HAS COME FOR ME TO PLAY MY PART, TOO!

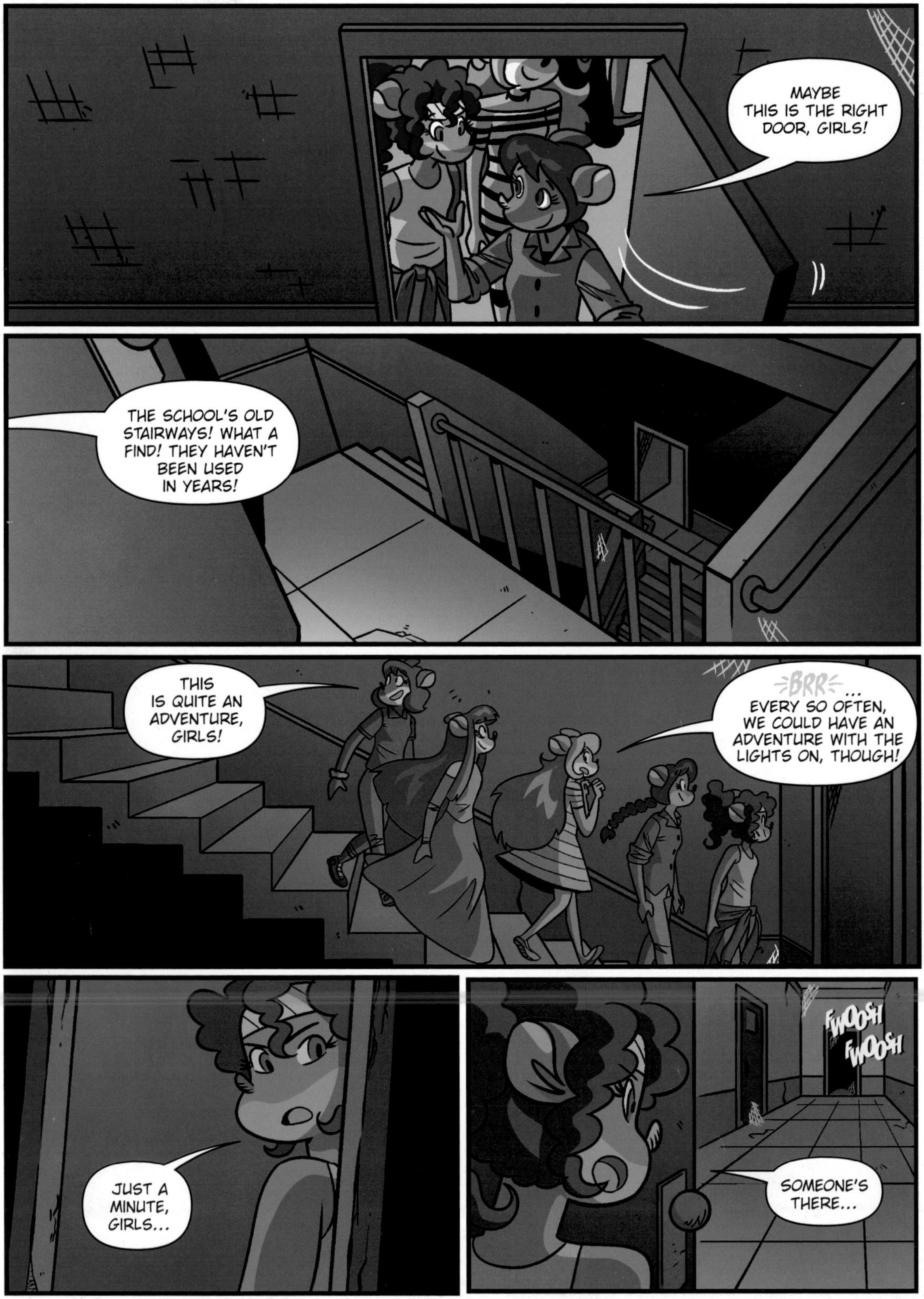
MAYBE THIS IS THE RIGHT DOOR, GIRLS!
THE SCHOOL'S OLD STAIRWAYS! WHAT A FIND! THEY HAVEN'T BEEN USED IN YEARS!
THIS IS QUITE AN ADVENTURE, GIRLS!
BRR... EVERY SO OFTEN, WE COULD HAVE AN ADVENTURE WITH THE LIGHTS ON, THOUGH!
JUST A MINUTE, GIRLS...
FWOOSH
FWOOSH
SOMEONE'S THERE...

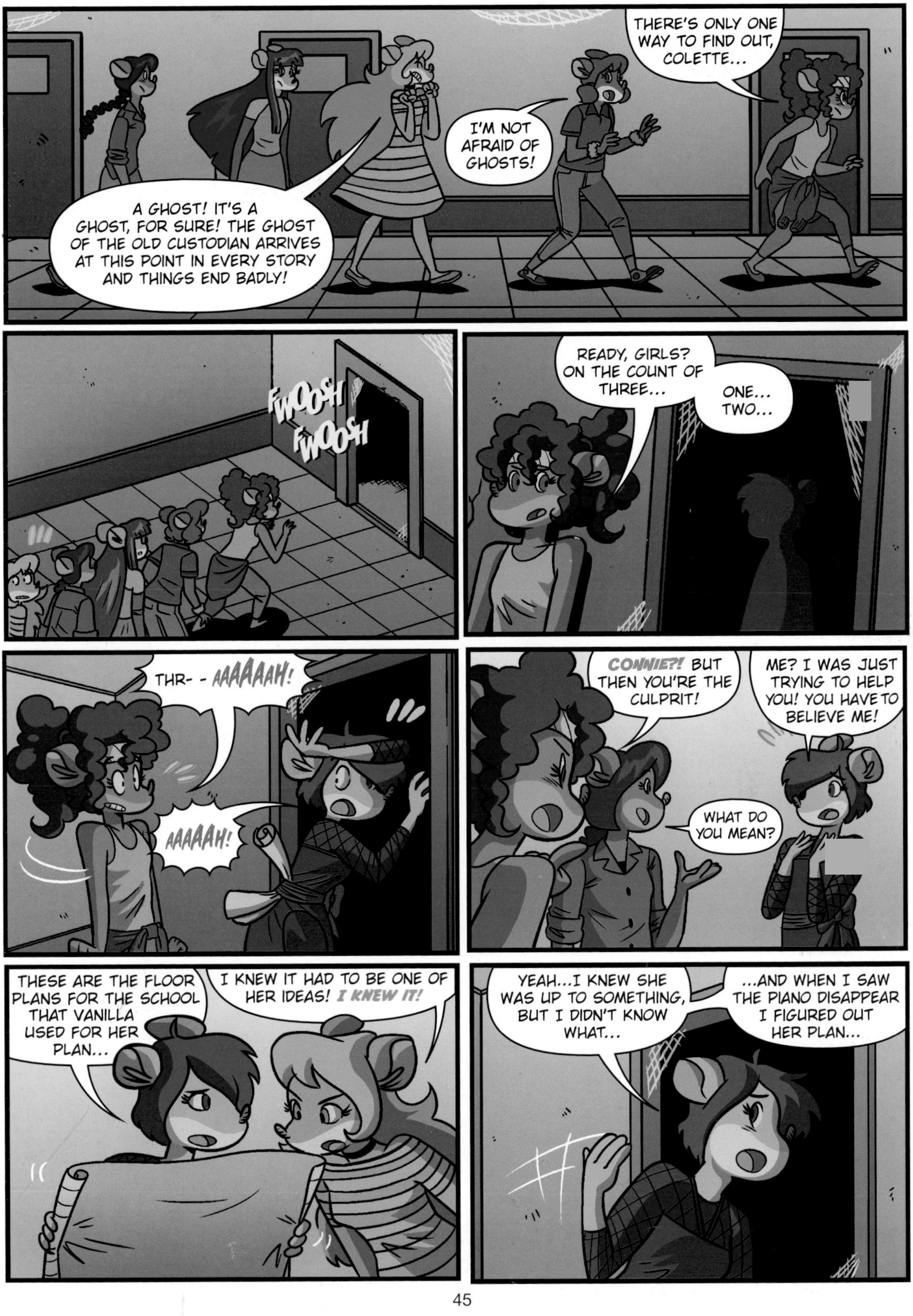
A GHOST! IT'S A GHOST, FOR SURE! THE GHOST OF THE OLD CUSTODIAN ARRIVES AT THIS POINT IN EVERY STORY AND THINGS END BADLY!
I'M NOT AFRAID OF GHOSTS!
THERE'S ONLY ONE WAY TO FIND OUT, COLETTE...
FWOOSH
FWOOSH
READY, GIRLS? ON THE COUNT OF THREE...
ONE... TWO...
THR- - AAAAAAH!
AAAAAH!
CONNIE?! BUT THEN YOU'RE THE CULPRIT!
ME? I WAS JUST TRYING TO HELP YOU! YOU HAVE TO BELIEVE ME!
WHAT DO YOU MEAN?
THESE ARE THE FLOOR PLANS FOR THE SCHOOL THAT VANILLA USED FOR HER PLAN...
I KNEW IT HAD TO BE ONE OF HER IDEAS! I KNEW IT!
YEAH...I KNEW SHE WAS UP TO SOMETHING, BUT I DIDN'T KNOW WHAT...
...AND WHEN I SAW THE PIANO DISAPPEAR I FIGURED OUT HER PLAN...

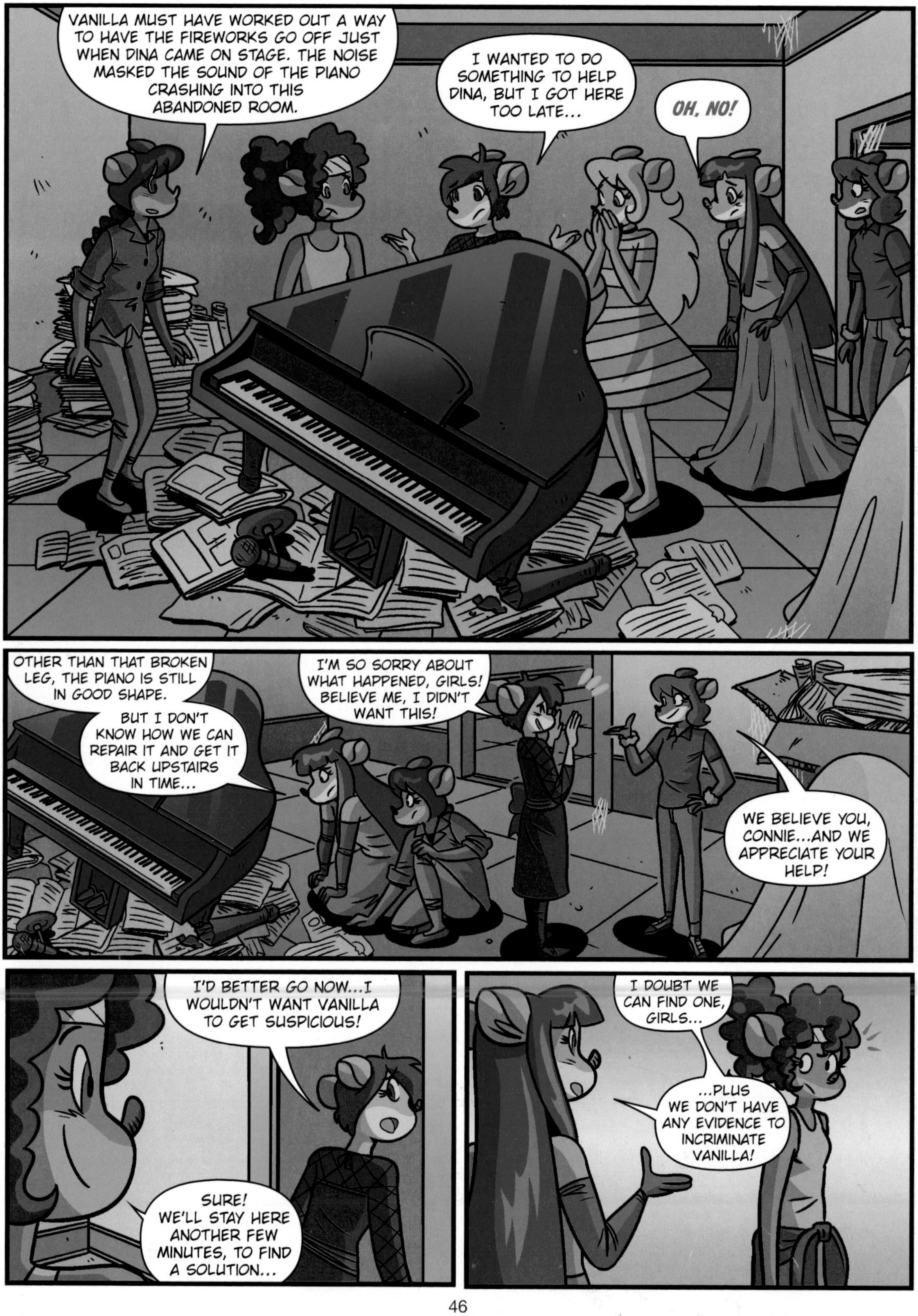
VANILLA MUST HAVE WORKED OUT A WAY TO HAVE THE FIREWORKS GO OFF JUST WHEN DINA CAME ON STAGE. THE NOISE MASKED THE SOUND OF THE PIANO CRASHING INTO THIS ABANDONED ROOM.
I WANTED TO DO SOMETHING TO HELP DINA, BUT I GOT HERE TOO LATE...
OH, NO!
OTHER THAN THAT BROKEN LEG, THE PIANO IS STILL IN GOOD SHAPE.
BUT I DON'T KNOW HOW WE CAN REPAIR IT AND GET IT BACK UPSTAIRS IN TIME...
I'M SO SORRY ABOUT WHAT HAPPENED, GIRLS! BELIEVE ME, I DIDN'T WANT THIS!
WE BELIEVE YOU, CONNIE...AND WE APPRECIATE YOUR HELP!
I'D BETTER GO NOW...I WOULDN'T WANT VANILLA TO GET SUSPICIOUS!
SURE! WE'LL STAY HERE ANOTHER FEW MINUTES, TO FIND A SOLUTION...
I DOUBT WE CAN FIND ONE, GIRLS...
...PLUS WE DON'T HAVE ANY EVIDENCE TO INCRIMINATE VANILLA!

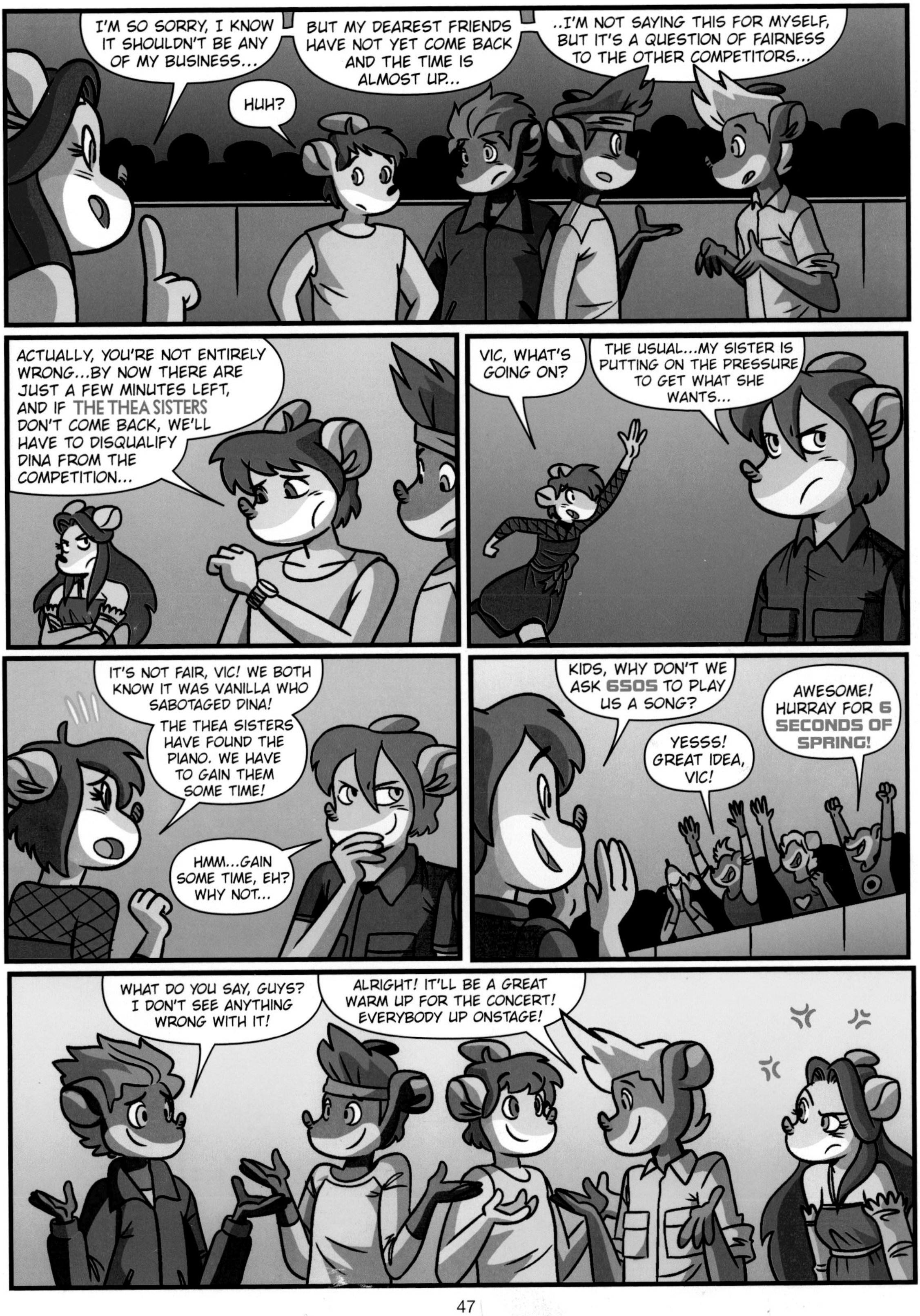
I'M SO SORRY, I KNOW IT SHOULDN'T BE ANY OF MY BUSINESS...
BUT MY DEAREST FRIENDS HAVE NOT YET COME BACK AND THE TIME IS ALMOST UP...
..I'M NOT SAYING THIS FOR MYSELF, BUT IT'S A QUESTION OF FAIRNESS TO THE OTHER COMPETITORS...
HUH?
ACTUALLY, YOU'RE NOT ENTIRELY WRONG...BY NOW THERE ARE JUST A FEW MINUTES LEFT, AND IF THE THEA SISTERS DON'T COME BACK, WE'LL HAVE TO DISQUALIFY DINA FROM THE COMPETITION...
VIC, WHAT'S GOING ON?
THE USUAL...MY SISTER IS PUTTING ON THE PRESSURE TO GET WHAT SHE WANTS...
IT'S NOT FAIR, VIC! WE BOTH KNOW IT WAS VANILLA WHO SABOTAGED DINA!
THE THEA SISTERS HAVE FOUND THE PIANO. WE HAVE TO GAIN THEM SOME TIME!
HMM...GAIN SOME TIME, EH? WHY NOT...
KIDS, WHY DON'T WE ASK 6SOS TO PLAY US A SONG?
YESSS! GREAT IDEA, VIC!
AWESOME! HURRAY FOR 6 SECONDS OF SPRING!
WHAT DO YOU SAY, GUYS? I DON'T SEE ANYTHING WRONG WITH IT!
ALRIGHT! IT'LL BE A GREAT WARM UP FOR THE CONCERT! EVERYBODY UP ONSTAGE!

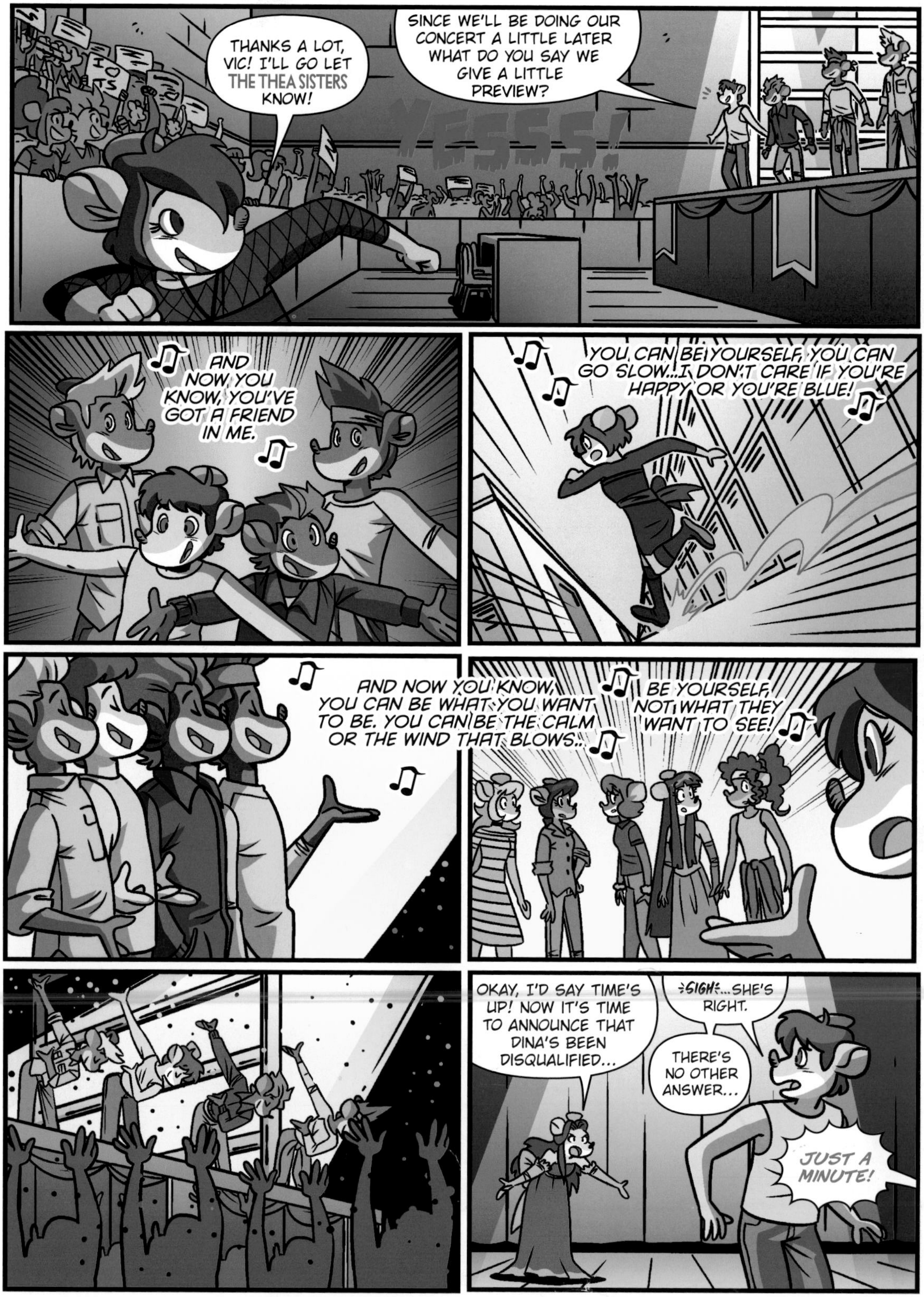
THANKS A LOT, VIC! I'LL GO LET THE THEA SISTERS KNOW!
SINCE WE'LL BE DOING OUR CONCERT A LITTLE LATER WHAT DO YOU SAY WE GIVE A LITTLE PREVIEW?
YESSS!
AND NOW YOU KNOW, YOU'VE GOT A FRIEND IN ME.
YOU CAN BE YOURSELF, YOU CAN GO SLOW...I DON'T CARE IF YOU'RE HAPPY OR YOU'RE BLUE!
AND NOW YOU KNOW, YOU CAN BE WHAT YOU WANT TO BE. YOU CAN BE THE CALM OR THE WIND THAT BLOWS...
BE YOURSELF, NOT WHAT THEY WANT TO SEE!
OKAY, I'D SAY TIME'S UP! NOW IT'S TIME TO ANNOUNCE THAT DINA'S BEEN DISQUALIFIED...
SIGH ...SHE'S RIGHT.
THERE'S NO OTHER ANSWER...
JUST A MINUTE!

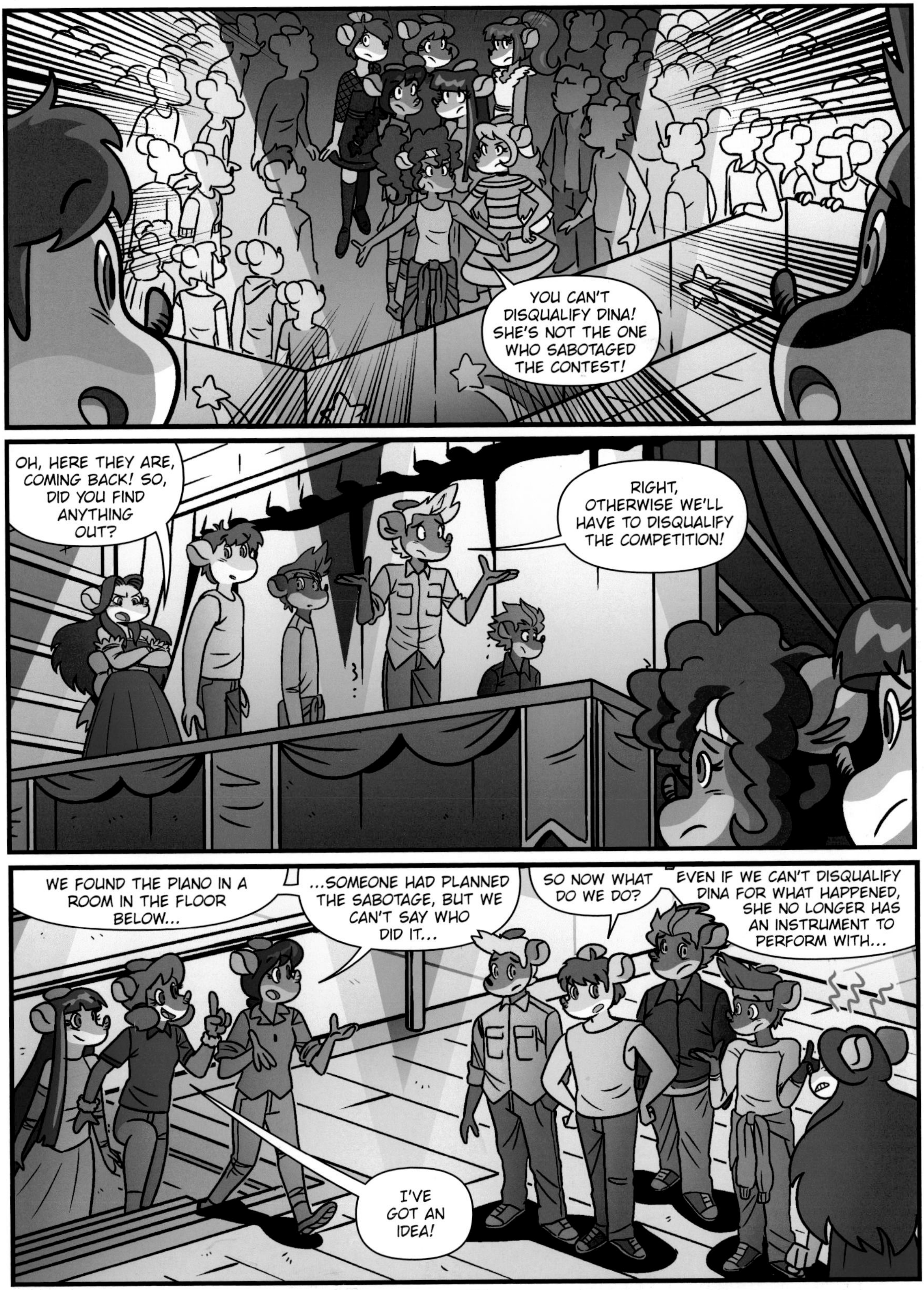
YOU CAN'T DISQUALIFY DINA! SHE'S NOT THE ONE WHO SABOTAGED THE CONTEST!
OH, HERE THEY ARE, COMING BACK! SO, DID YOU FIND ANYTHING OUT?
RIGHT, OTHERWISE WE'LL HAVE TO DISQUALIFY THE COMPETITION!
WE FOUND THE PIANO IN A ROOM IN THE FLOOR BELOW...
...SOMEONE HAD PLANNED THE SABOTAGE, BUT WE CAN'T SAY WHO DID IT...
SO NOW WHAT DO WE DO?
EVEN IF WE CAN'T DISQUALIFY DINA FOR WHAT HAPPENED, SHE NO LONGER HAS AN INSTRUMENT TO PERFORM WITH...
I'VE GOT AN IDEA!

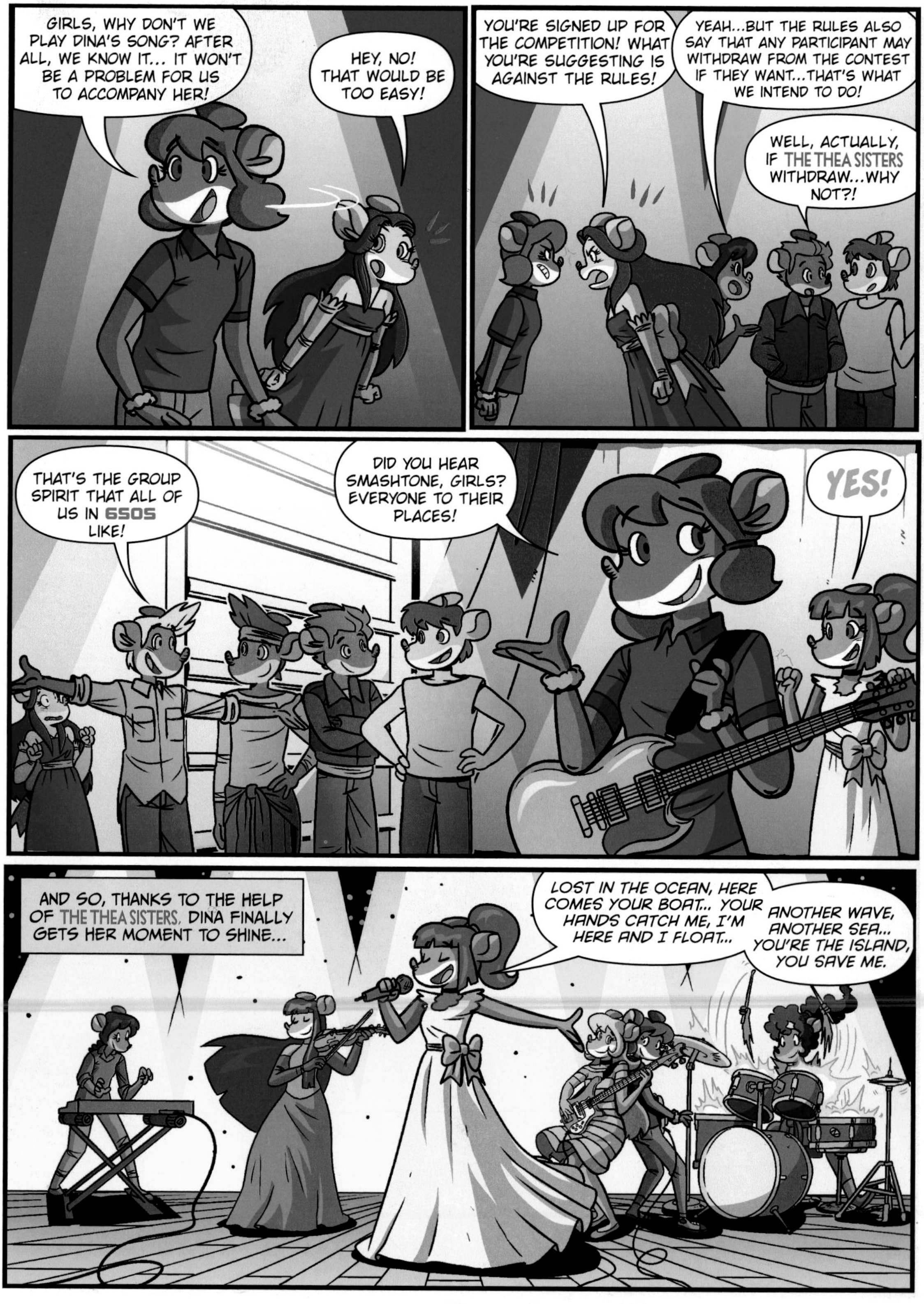
GIRLS, WHY DON'T WE PLAY DINA'S SONG? AFTER ALL, WE KNOW IT... IT WON'T BE A PROBLEM FOR US TO ACCOMPANY HER!
HEY, NO! THAT WOULD BE TOO EASY!
YOU'RE SIGNED UP FOR THE COMPETITION! WHAT YOU'RE SUGGESTING IS AGAINST THE RULES!
YEAH...BUT THE RULES ALSO SAY THAT ANY PARTICIPANT MAY WITHDRAW FROM THE CONTEST IF THEY WANT...THAT'S WHAT WE INTEND TO DO!
WELL, ACTUALLY, IF THE THEA SISTERS WITHDRAW...WHY NOT?!
THAT'S THE GROUP SPIRIT THAT ALL OF US IN 650S LIKE!
DID YOU HEAR SMASHTONE, GIRLS? EVERYONE TO THEIR PLACES!
YES!
AND SO, THANKS TO THE HELP OF THE THEA SISTERS, DINA FINALLY GETS HER MOMENT TO SHINE...
LOST IN THE OCEAN, HERE COMES YOUR BOAT... YOUR HANDS CATCH ME, I'M HERE AND I FLOAT...
ANOTHER WAVE, ANOTHER SEA... YOU'RE THE ISLAND, YOU SAVE ME.

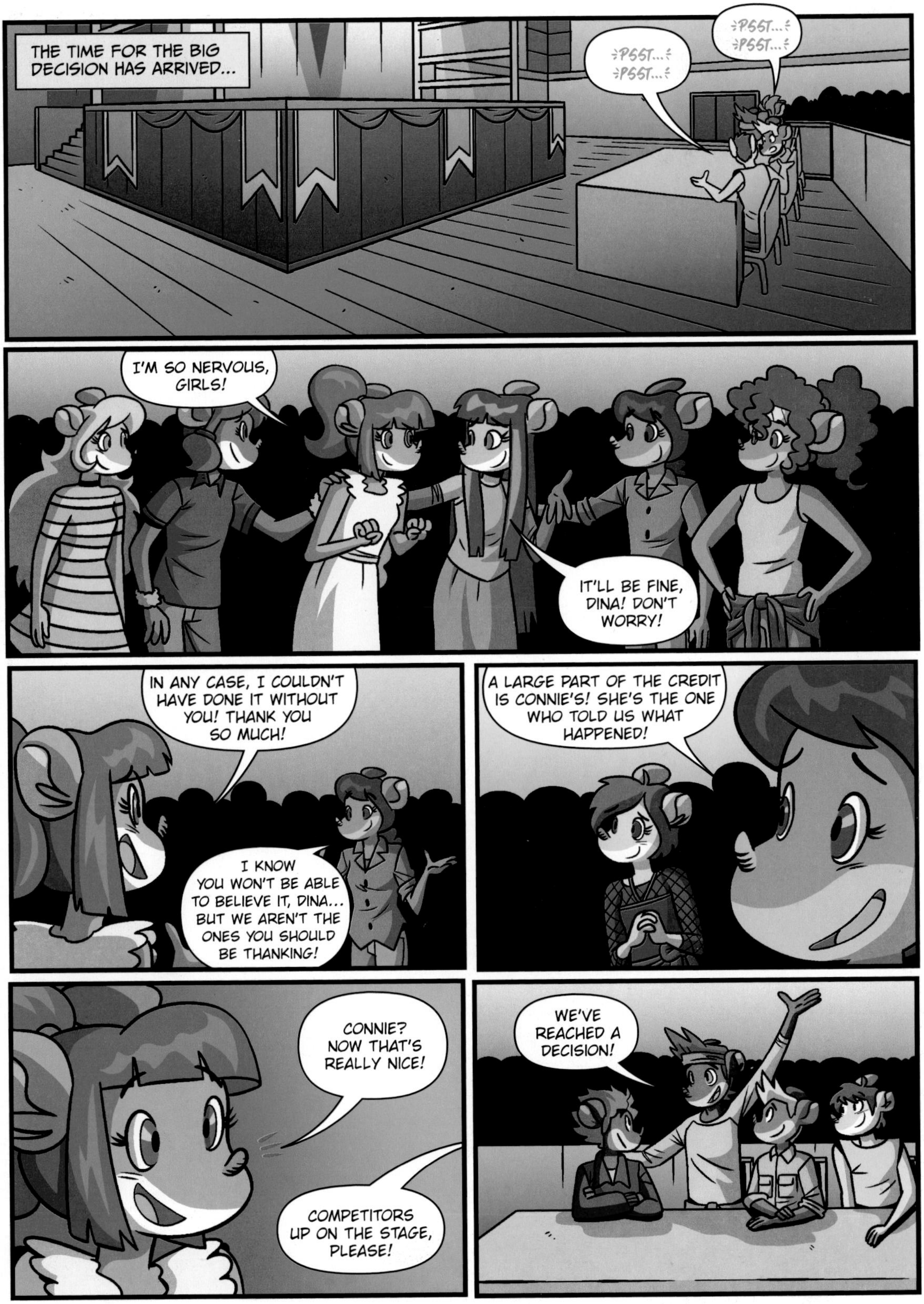
THE TIME FOR THE BIG DECISION HAS ARRIVED...
PSST... PSST...
PSST... PSST...
I'M SO NERVOUS, GIRLS!
IT'LL BE FINE, DINA! DON'T WORRY!
IN ANY CASE, I COULDN'T HAVE DONE IT WITHOUT YOU! THANK YOU SO MUCH!
I KNOW YOU WON'T BE ABLE TO BELIEVE IT, DINA... BUT WE AREN'T THE ONES YOU SHOULD BE THANKING!
A LARGE PART OF THE CREDIT IS CONNIE'S! SHE'S THE ONE WHO TOLD US WHAT HAPPENED!
CONNIE? NOW THAT'S REALLY NICE!
COMPETITORS UP ON THE STAGE, PLEASE!
WE'VE REACHED A DECISION!

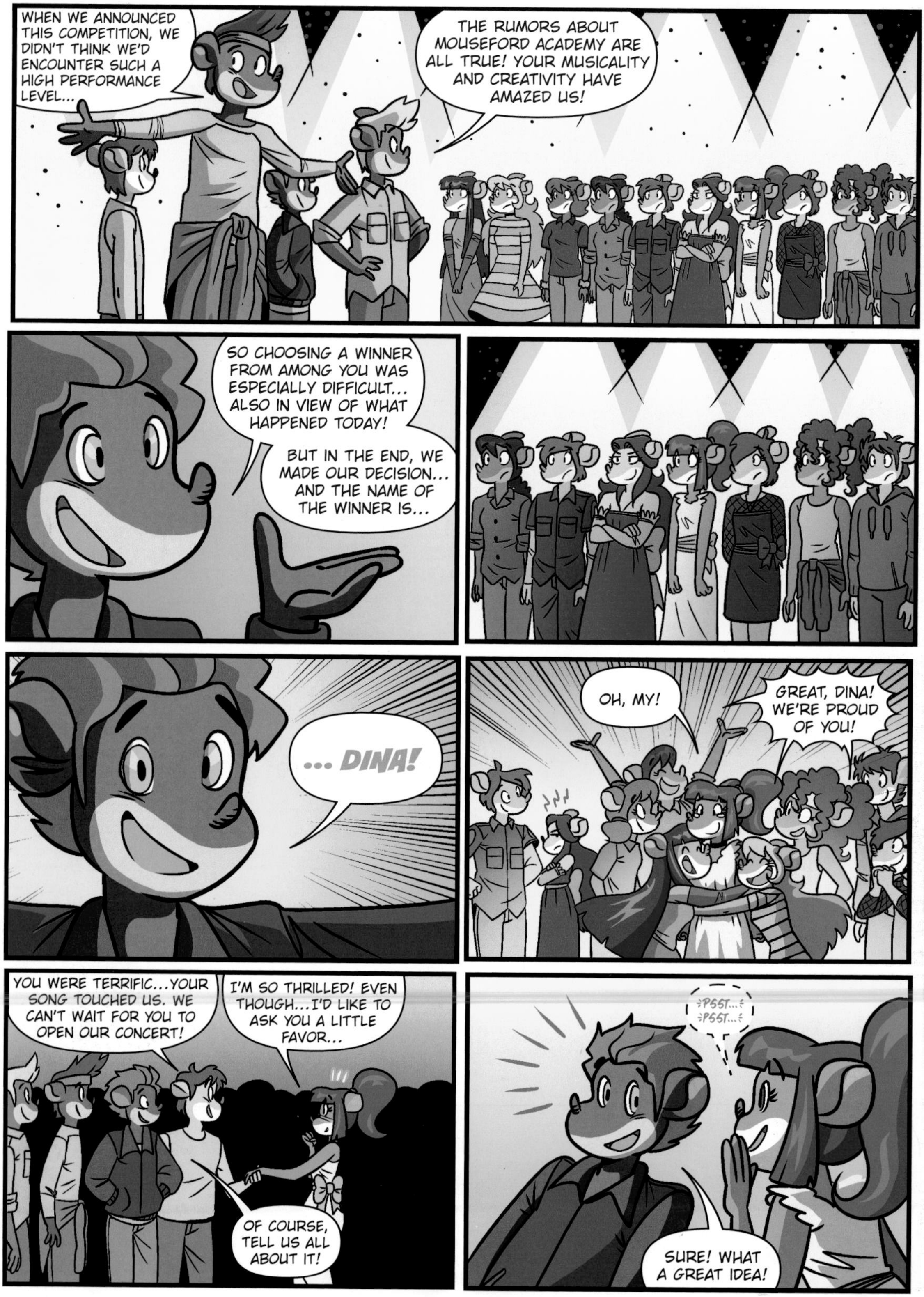
WHEN WE ANNOUNCED THIS COMPETITION, WE DIDN'T THINK WE'D ENCOUNTER SUCH A HIGH PERFORMANCE LEVEL...
THE RUMORS ABOUT MOUSEFORD ACADEMY ARE ALL TRUE! YOUR MUSICALITY AND CREATIVITY HAVE AMAZED US!
SO CHOOSING A WINNER FROM AMONG YOU WAS ESPECIALLY DIFFICULT... ALSO IN VIEW OF WHAT HAPPENED TODAY!
BUT IN THE END, WE MADE OUR DECISION... AND THE NAME OF THE WINNER IS...
... DINA!
OH, MY!
GREAT, DINA! WE'RE PROUD OF YOU!
YOU WERE TERRIFIC... YOUR SONG TOUCHED US. WE CAN'T WAIT FOR YOU TO OPEN OUR CONCERT!
I'M SO THRILLED! EVEN THOUGH... I'D LIKE TO ASK YOU A LITTLE FAVOR...
OF COURSE, TELL US ALL ABOUT IT!
PSST... PSST...
SURE! WHAT A GREAT IDEA!

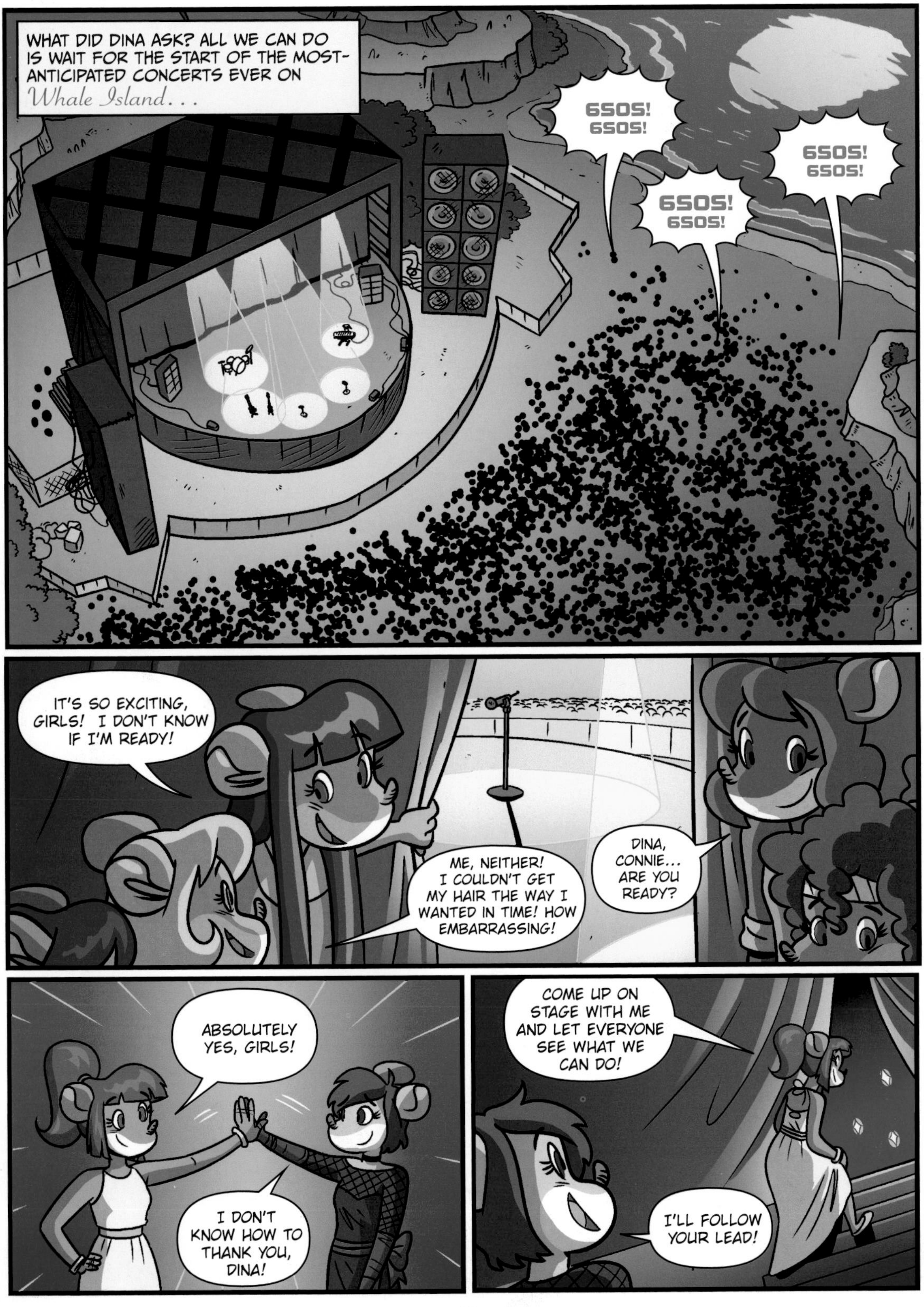
WHAT DID DINA ASK? ALL WE CAN DO IS WAIT FOR THE START OF THE MOST-ANTICIPATED CONCERTS EVER ON Whale Island...
6SOS! 6SOS!
6SOS! 6SOS!
6SOS! 6SOS!
IT'S SO EXCITING, GIRLS! I DON'T KNOW IF I'M READY!
ME, NEITHER! I COULDN'T GET MY HAIR THE WAY I WANTED IN TIME! HOW EMBARRASSING!
DINA, CONNIE... ARE YOU READY?
ABSOLUTELY YES, GIRLS!
I DON'T KNOW HOW TO THANK YOU, DINA!
COME UP ON STAGE WITH ME AND LET EVERYONE SEE WHAT WE CAN DO!
I'LL FOLLOW YOUR LEAD!

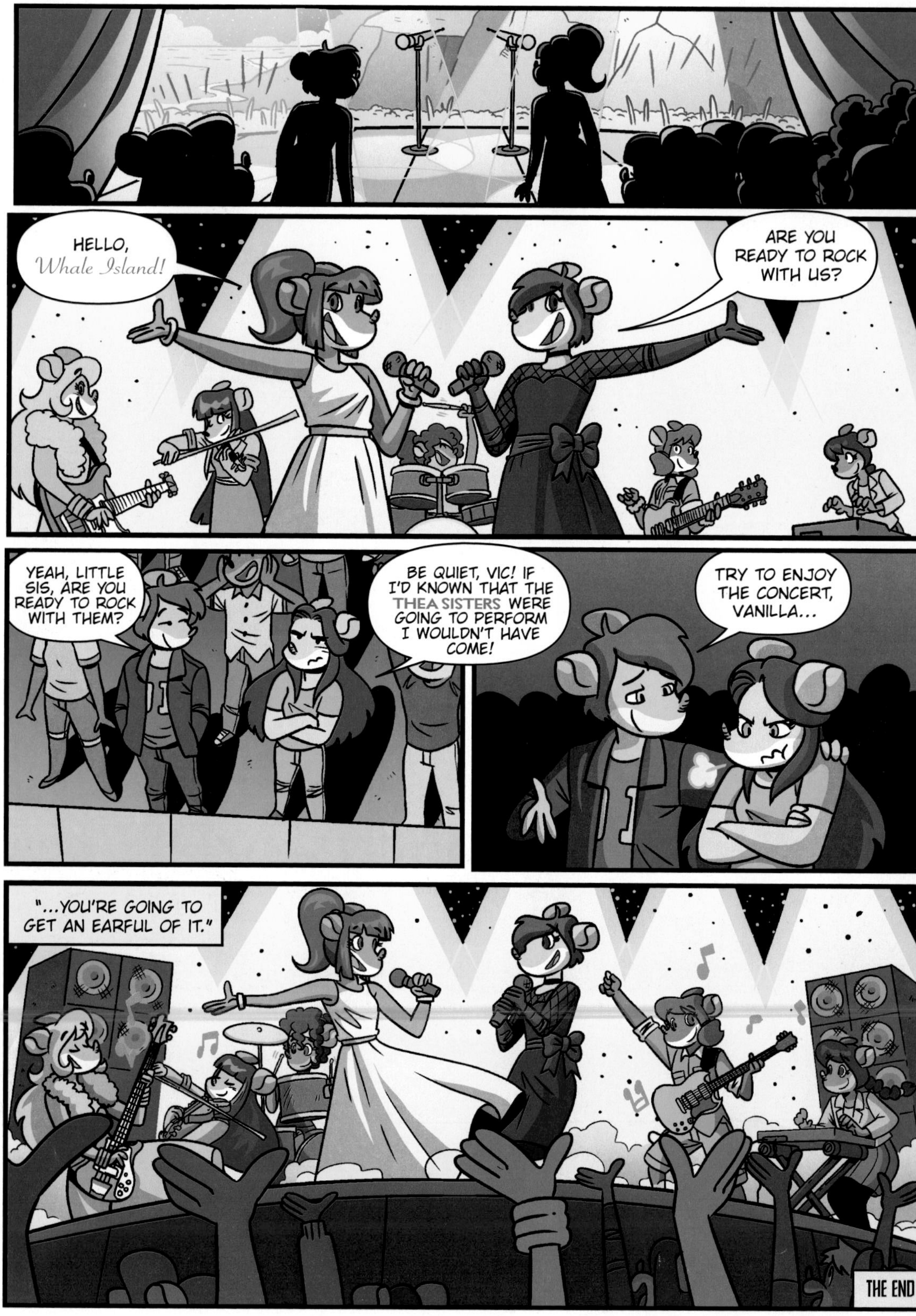
HELLO, Whale Island!
ARE YOU READY TO ROCK WITH US?
YEAH, LITTLE SIS, ARE YOU READY TO ROCK WITH THEM?
BE QUIET, VIC! IF I'D KNOWN THAT THE THEA SISTERS WERE GOING TO PERFORM I WOULDN'T HAVE COME!
TRY TO ENJOY THE CONCERT, VANILLA...
"...YOU'RE GOING TO GET AN EARFUL OF IT."
THE END

Watch Out For PAPERCUTZ™

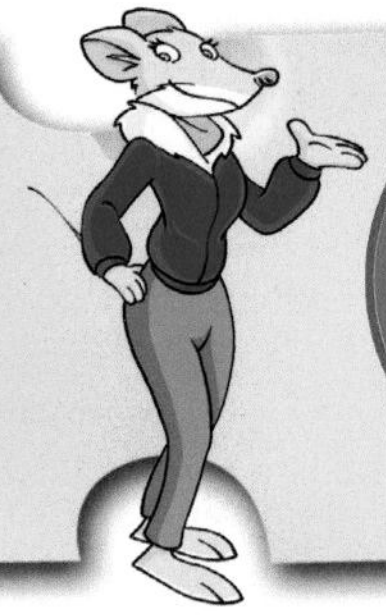

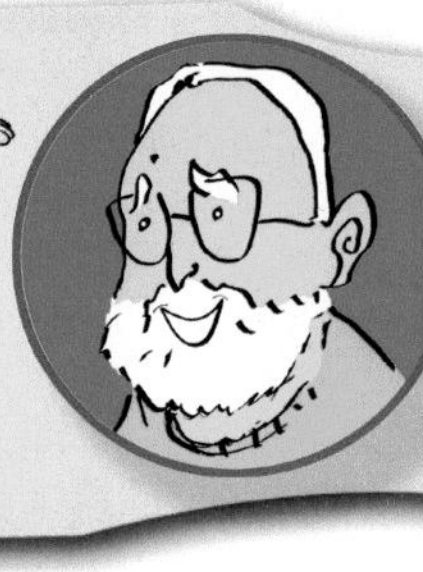

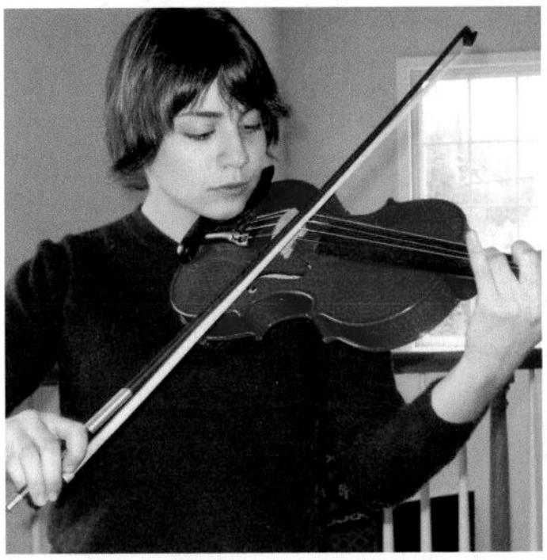

Photo by Diana Fawaz Kimiatek

Welcome to the song-filled, soundless seventh THEA STILTON graphic novel reported by Thea Stilton (as told to Francesco Savino, writer, and Ryan Jampole, artist) from Papercutz, that mixed bag of musicians and non-musicians that are dedicated to publishing great graphic novels for all ages. I'm Salicrup, *Jim Salicrup,* the rhythmically-challenged Editor-in-Chief and one-time piano student. Our publisher, Terry Nantier, plays drums, and our newest Production Coordinator, Sasha Kimiatek plays violin. We're not sure if any other members of the Papercutz staff or the THEA STILTON creative team play musical instruments, but we'll ask them and report our findings in THEA STILTON #8.

To back up a bit, let me once again offer a quick explanation of this graphic novel series. As Thea Stilton herself spells out on our inside front cover, Thea is a special correspondent to the Rodent's Gazette, the most famouse newspaper on Mouse Island, and she also teaches journalism at Mouseford Academy, where she got to know five very special students—Colette, Nicky, Pamela, Paulina, and Violet—who formed the Thea Sisters, a group inspired by and named after her. So not only do the girls aspire to be top-notch journalists, they also know how to rock, as shown in this very graphic novel. The confusing part about all this is that this series is called THEA STILTON, but she's rarely in the actual stories she's telling here. That's why we're trying to work "the Thea Sisters" into the titles now, to avoid any possible confusion. But as the girls prove in this issue, they're so talented, there's almost nothing they can't do.

But maybe we shouldn't be so surprised. Just last year, the Nobel Prize for Literature went to Bob Dylan—a musician! It was the lyrics he wrote that really garnered the award, as opposed to his guitar (or harmonica) playing or singing. So maybe the idea of five journalism students forming a band isn't so crazy after all? It all comes down to communication. While many pop songs may just be designed to simply be fun and entertaining, many songs also contain interesting little stories. Obviously love songs may express everything from simple declarations of love to complicated tales of romantic relationships. While some may have a true gift for song-writing, such as Dina, many of of us may be closer to Vanilla de Visssen, not to mention Harmony Smurf! (You know who he is, right? If not, check out any of THE SMURFS graphic novels from Papercutz.)

While in "The Watch Out For Papercutz" page in THEA STILTON #6 we talked about how difficult it may be for print journalists these days, many young people are perhaps writing more than ever—but on social media! Everyone seems to be texting each other, or posting on Facebook, or in the case of our newest president—Tweeting! The point is, almost everyone has become a journalist to some extent. Unfortunately, not everyone studies to be a journalist, so what's reported on social media shouldn't be trusted to necessarily be the truth. Then again, even the most respected journalists are routinely accused of being biased these days. Finding the truth can be quite a struggle sometimes. But fortunately, there are still many like the Thea Sisters, Thea Stilton, and (her brother and Editor of The Rodent's Gazette) Geronimo Stilton devoted to trying to report the truth and serve society by keeping us well-informed on what's going on in the world.

If all of the above sounds to you like we have a lot of respect for journalists, you're right. Many of the best have risked their lives to be able to tell us the truth at very important times in history, some have actually helped change history for the better. If, like the Thea Sisters, you're thinking about becoming a journalist, we wish you the very best of luck! (Of course we support anything that you aspire to be—as there are so many wonderful careers you can choose from!)

And then there's us-- comicbook makers dedicated to telling stories that we hope entertain you, and maybe, sometimes inspire you.

Thanks,

JIM

Stay in Touch!

Email: salicrup@papercutz.com
Web: www.papercutz.com
Twitter: @papercutzgn
Facebook: PAPERCUTZGRAPHICNOVELS
Snailmail: Papercutz, 160 Broadway, Suite 700, East Wing, New York, NY 10038

Geronimo Stilton

GRAPHIC NOVELS AVAILABLE FROM

PAPERCUTZ™

...ALSO AVAILABLE WHEREVER E-BOOKS ARE SOLD!

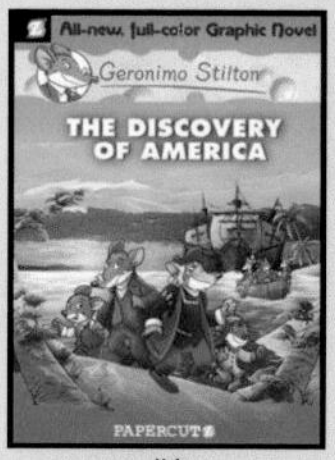
All-new, full-color Graphic Novel
Geronimo Stilton
THE DISCOVERY OF AMERICA
PAPERCUTZ

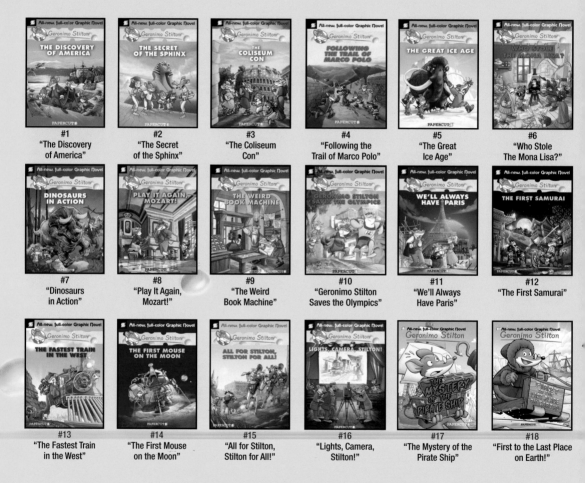

#1 "The Discovery of America"

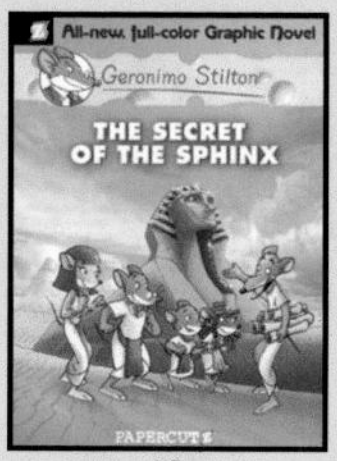
All-new, full-color Graphic Novel
Geronimo Stilton
THE SECRET OF THE SPHINX
PAPERCUTZ

#2 "The Secret of the Sphinx"

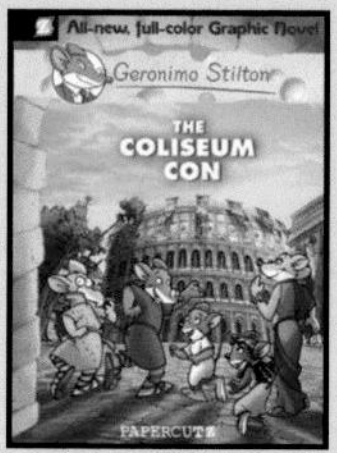
All-new, full-color Graphic Novel
Geronimo Stilton
THE COLISEUM CON
PAPERCUTZ

#3 "The Coliseum Con"

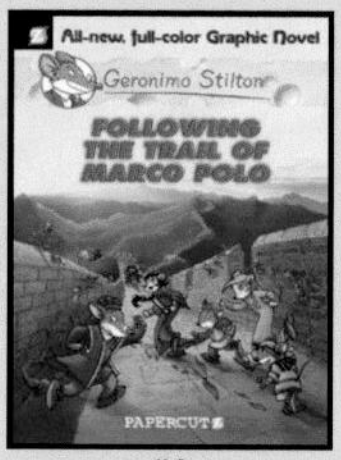
All-new, full-color Graphic Novel
Geronimo Stilton
FOLLOWING THE TRAIL OF MARCO POLO
PAPERCUTZ

#4 "Following the Trail of Marco Polo"

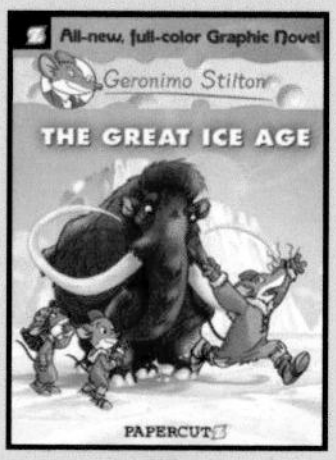
All-new, full-color Graphic Novel
Geronimo Stilton
THE GREAT ICE AGE
PAPERCUTZ

#5 "The Great Ice Age"

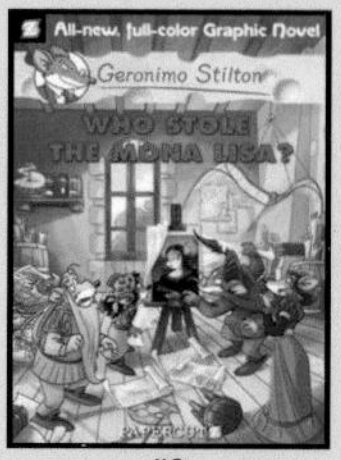
All-new, full-color Graphic Novel
Geronimo Stilton
WHO STOLE THE MONA LISA?

#6 "Who Stole The Mona Lisa?"

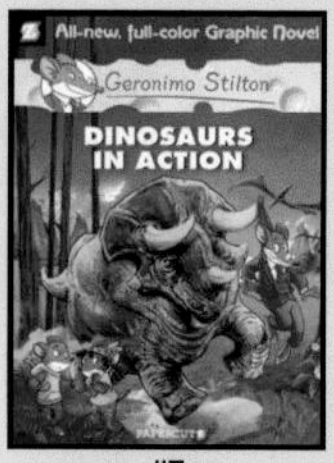
All-new, full-color Graphic Novel
Geronimo Stilton
DINOSAURS IN ACTION
PAPERCUTZ

#7 "Dinosaurs in Action"

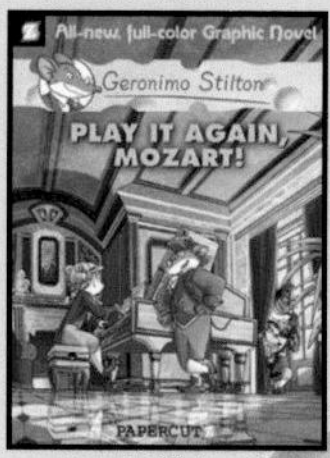
All-new, full-color Graphic Novel
Geronimo Stilton
PLAY IT AGAIN, MOZART!
PAPERCUTZ

#8 "Play It Again, Mozart!"

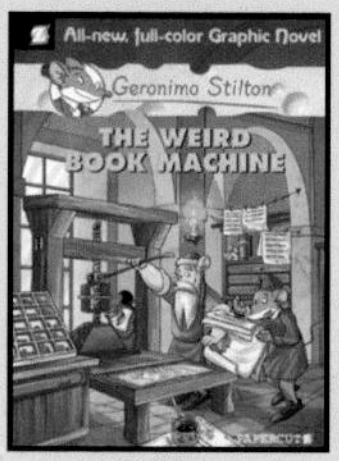
All-new, full-color Graphic Novel
Geronimo Stilton
THE WEIRD BOOK MACHINE
PAPERCUTZ

#9 "The Weird Book Machine"

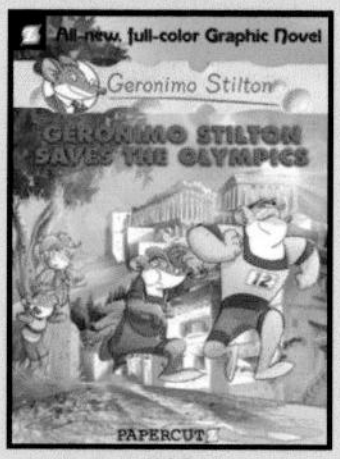
All-new, full-color Graphic Novel
Geronimo Stilton
GERONIMO STILTON SAVES THE OLYMPICS
PAPERCUTZ

#10 "Geronimo Stilton Saves the Olympics"

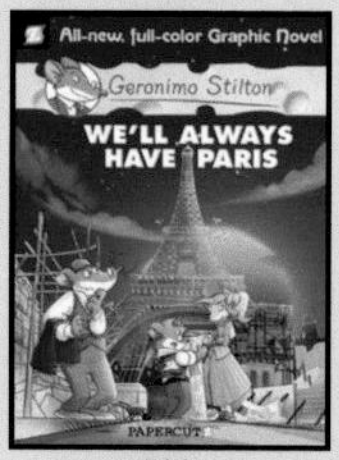
All-new, full-color Graphic Novel
Geronimo Stilton
WE'LL ALWAYS HAVE PARIS
PAPERCUTZ

#11 "We'll Always Have Paris"

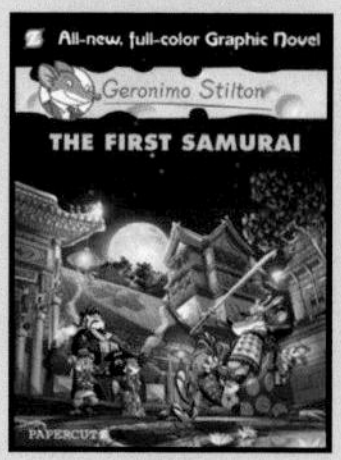
All-new, full-color Graphic Novel
Geronimo Stilton
THE FIRST SAMURAI
PAPERCUTZ

#12 "The First Samurai"

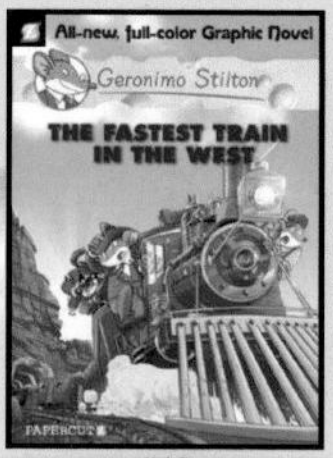
All-new, full-color Graphic Novel
Geronimo Stilton
THE FASTEST TRAIN IN THE WEST
PAPERCUTZ

#13 "The Fastest Train in the West"

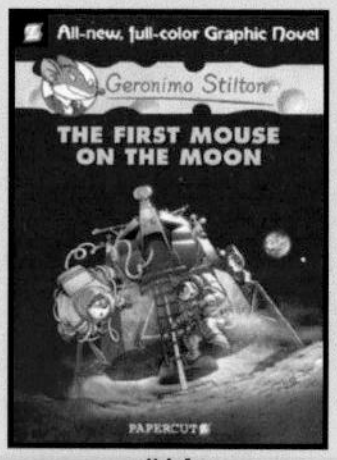
All-new, full-color Graphic Novel
Geronimo Stilton
THE FIRST MOUSE ON THE MOON
PAPERCUTZ

#14 "The First Mouse on the Moon"

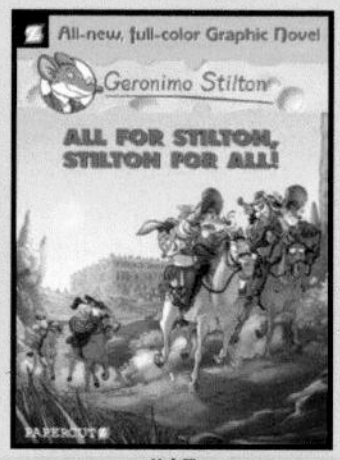
All-new, full-color Graphic Novel
Geronimo Stilton
ALL FOR STILTON, STILTON FOR ALL!
PAPERCUTZ

#15 "All for Stilton, Stilton for All!"

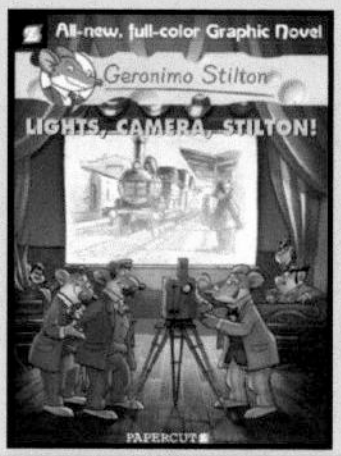
All-new, full-color Graphic Novel
Geronimo Stilton
LIGHTS, CAMERA, STILTON!
PAPERCUTZ

#16 "Lights, Camera, Stilton!"

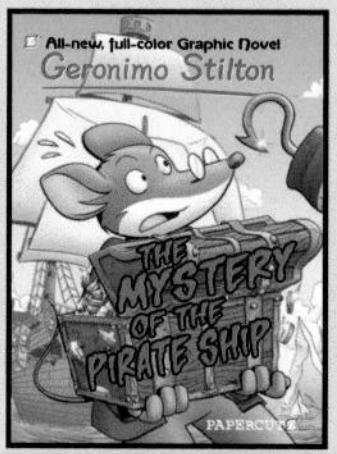
All-new, full-color Graphic Novel
Geronimo Stilton
THE MYSTERY OF THE PIRATE SHIP
PAPERCUTZ

#17 "The Mystery of the Pirate Ship"

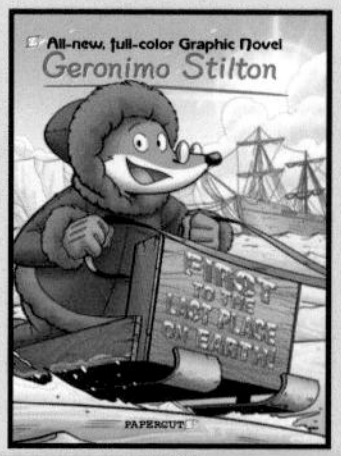
All-new, full-color Graphic Novel
Geronimo Stilton
PAPERCUTZ

#18 "First to the Last Place on Earth!"

papercutz.com

GERONIMO STILTON graphic novels are available for $9.99 each only in hardcover. Available from booksellers everywhere. You can also order online from papercutz.com. Or call 1-800-886-1223, Monday through Friday, 9 – 5 EST. MC, Visa, and AmEx accepted. To order by mail, please add $4.00 for postage and handling for first book ordered, $1.00 for each additional book and make check payable to NBM Publishing.

Send to: Papercutz, 160 Broadway, Suite 700, East Wing, New York, NY 10038.

Vanilla de Vissen
is the daughter of the queen of cosmetics, Vissia de Vissen. Spoiled and capricious, she's very jealous of the Thea Sisters!

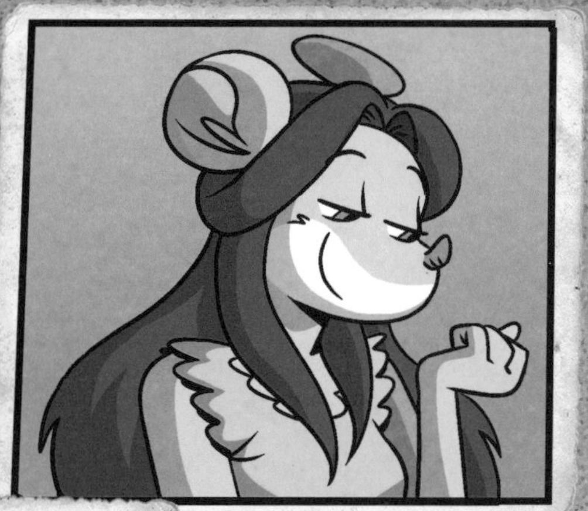

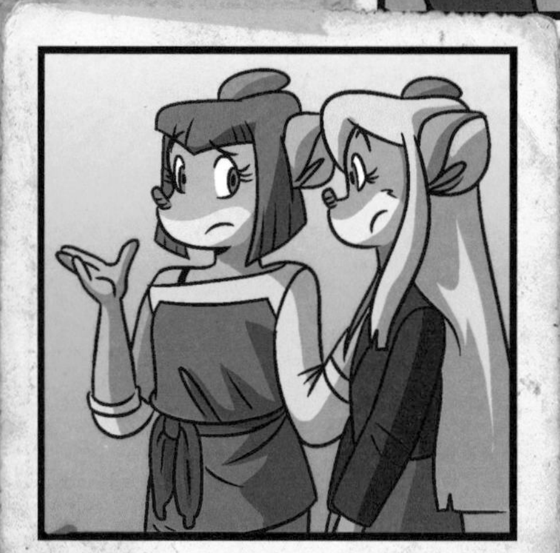

Zoe and Alicia
are Vanilla's friends who will follow her every move and aid in every scheme.

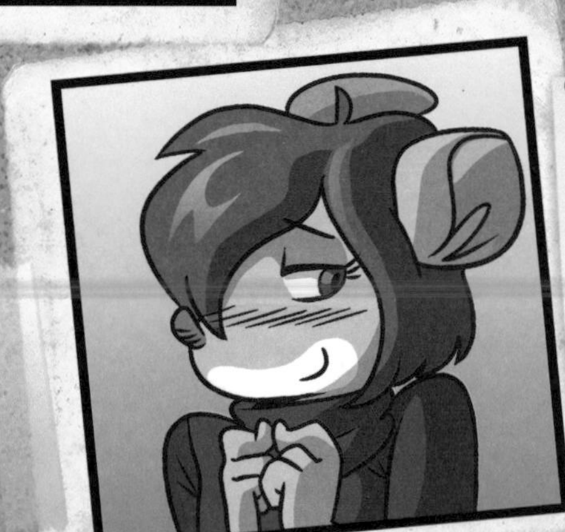

Connie
is also a friend of Vanilla's. But is she realizing Vanilla's intentions are not always noble?

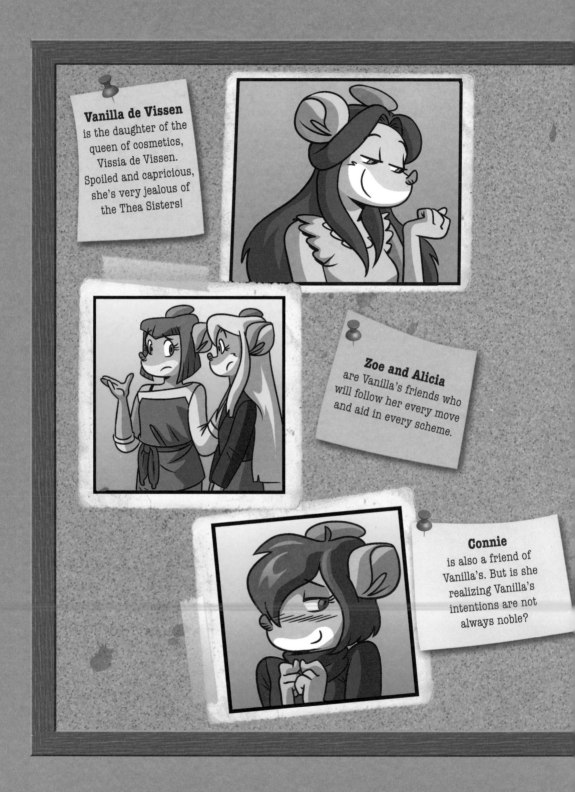